The Ultimate Alternative:

When One Chooses Lust Over Love

By Richard Watkins

Edited, Designed, and Published by:

Desktop Prepress Services
Donna L. Ferrier
808 S. New Bethel Blvd.
Ada, OK 74820
1-866-220-4160
http://www.desktopprepress.com

Cover photo and chapter header photos © James Steidl, Jgroup, San Diego, California

Other inside graphics © 2009 Jupiter Images

Scripture taken from the HOLY BIBLE, NEW INTERNATIONAL VERSION®. Copyright © 1973, 1978, 1984 International Bible Society. Used by permission of Zondervan. All rights reserved.

Printed in the United States of America.

ISBN 978-0-578-02469-1

Table of Contents

ver wonder why so many relationships, even those that begin on a healthy note, ultimately end in turmoil? One of the most common reasons is people choosing lust over love, and this happens far more often than most of us realize. *The Ultimate Alternative: When One Chooses Lust Over Love* examines the myriad of reasons why people make such a disastrous choice and end up ruining what could have been a healthy relationship.

The Ultimate Alternative is a novel that employs fictional characters to tell a story. While the characters are fictitious, the story is true. *The Ultimate Alternative* highlights some of the most exciting moments in our lives, and at the same time, examines poor decisions most of us have made regarding relationships. *The Ultimate Alternative* will bring readers to the edge of their seats in laughter, adventure, and mystery in the triangle of love that many people have found themselves in, all because they chose lust over love.

Regardless of gender, race, or sexual preference, many of us have been faced with the temptation that lust has to offer. Unfortunately, many of us act on that temptation. That's one of the many reasons readers will be able to relate to most, if not all, the characters in this story. They may represent those near and dear to us.

The Ultimate Alternative also deals with some sensitive and deeply personal relational issues. For generations, men have been allowed to have as many women as they need to fulfill their lusts at their own convenience, while women are expected to find one man to call a "husband." Unfortunately, many women today are turning into what men have been for years---pimps! *The Ultimate Alternative* paints a picture of the trickery such women are capable of, causing nothing but confusion, violence, and rage in the men they claim to love. Fact is, many men are victimized and even assaulted in dating relationships, all because the relationships are rooted in lust. *The Ultimate Alternative* shows its readers how to recognize lust by its unstable, unhealthy rollercoaster rides of emotion that don't occur in healthy relationships deeply rooted in love.

Lastly, this story will force readers to think twice about the most important elements in a relationship and the consequences of choosing lust over love. It will force a person to be cognizant of making the right choices when faced with the temptation to become immorally involved with someone. If you're in a meaningful relationship with someone who has great attributes, don't ever take that person for granted, and don't ever think that someone else isn't waiting for an opportunity to take your place with your mate, even if it's only for one night. One does not necessarily have to be in a night club environment to find oneself in a situation that will require them to make sound and moral decisions.

Even though the novel is geared toward young adults, people of all ages will be able to understand and appreciate its message. In all likelihood, you've either been through the experiences depicted in this novel or you know someone who has. So sit back and allow you mind to relax and be as objective as possible as you read this story. It will make you laugh, think, and then laugh some more.

Acknowledgements

would like to acknowledge and thank a few people that have been a part of my life that have motivated me in writing this novel. First, I'd like to thank my greatest inspiration for all my accomplishments: My Lord and Savior Jesus Christ, for blessing me each and every day.

I'd also like to acknowledge my wonderful God-fearing parents, who raised me in an atmosphere of love, realistic upbringing, protection, and firm discipline. Because of their Godly influence, I've been able to graduate from private and public schools, colleges, academies, and other training institutions.

I'd also like to thank my older brother for paving the way for me as a youngster. From him, I learned how to make correct decisions just by observing his. In addition, his competitive nature will always bring out the best in me as well as his great brotherly love.

In addition, I'd like to thank my wonderful God-fearing wife for all the support that she has given me in writing this novel and being the backbone that every successful man should have.

Finally, 10 percent of the proceeds from the sale of this novel will be donated to the Church of Christ on North Clinton Avenue in Trenton, New Jersey.

Chapter 1

The Genesis of It All

t was the time of year when the sun set upon one's face. The air was pleasant, and the humidity was relatively low considering it was August. Families were enjoying cookouts, picnics, and even wild parties together. On this particular day, Isaac was at the top of his game. Isaac is an African American young man with the potential to accomplish great things in life. He would be an asset to any employer and a good father to any child he helped birth. Isaac is a natural leader and could achieve anything he set out to accomplish once he made up his mind. Isaac's medium build, chocolate complexion, well-muscled exterior, and innocent, boyish expression were eye candy for most women. Ladies went particularly crazy over his thick eyebrows and long eyelashes. He was also a snappy dresser, which always grabbed the attention of both men and women alike. Isaac had just graduated with a Bachelor's Degree in Public Administration and was an aspiring politician. His goal in life was to make a positive difference in his community, future family, and the world.

Isaac was dressed to impress at a cookout his friend Darius invited him to attend. He wore a pair of ivory dress slacks, tailor fitted with gold and beige alligator dress shoes, and a tailor-fitted, multi-colored gold silk dress shirt bearing at least half of his well-developed chest. And he always wore a white gold necklace of the Cross. That day he completed his GQ attire with a dress straw hat with the brim slanted across his left eyebrow.

He also always made a conscience effort to smell appealing. He wore the finest colognes on the market, and he knew how to mix and match them to create his own unique aroma that left a lasting impression on anyone around him. As Isaac entered Darius' backyard, time seemed to stand still for a few seconds as all eyes gazed upon Isaac in admiration. And even though he knew he was looking good, Isaac made a conscience effort to be as humble as possible. He always remembered the family values his parents instilled in him. One of those values was never to think he was better than anyone else and to not only love himself, but others as well. Isaac was very secure, confident, and mild-mannered all at the same time. He laid all that charm and personality on all the guests at the cookout, while he blessed them with his exuberating smile and a firm, but gentle, handshake. Isaac greeted everyone with a "Hello, how are you doing today?" in his signature monotone voice. Most people at the cookout couldn't wait to meet him. He knew how to work a room full of admirers as well as haters.

But, yes, there was a small group of individuals (mostly men) who were repulsed at the mere image of Isaac and the attention he was getting from most of the attractive women present. As a good judge of character, Isaac felt the negative vibes of the haters. He even introduced himself to them to try to let them know he was no threat because he didn't want anything they had. Darius came running from the kitchen to greet his Main Man, his Ace, his Partna' and his Dog! "What's happening, Pimp? Damn you did it again with the clothes, man; you got it on like lotion, partna," Darius said to Isaac as he shook his hand in love.

Darius was also an African American young man with a very promising future. He didn't go to college like Isaac did, but he was a General Manager for a reputable car dealership in Manhattan, New York, striving diligently to become an owner of a chain of five dealerships in the area. While Darius was considered by many to be good looking, he had a serious problem. Darius could not stay committed to his lovely wife. Every time he saw an attractive woman, he jumped at the opportunity to be with her in a way that violated his wedding vows. Unfortunately, Darius came across many sexy women in his line of work, and no matter how hard he tried to resist the temptation of a beautiful, athletic-looking woman, he failed miserably at maintaining a strictly professional relationship. Whether they were secretaries, assistant managers, CEOs in the industry, or even walk-in customers, Darius always found the forbidden avenue into their minds and then into their beds. Many who knew him considered him a pimp, not in the sense that he had a stock of women in a stable who he convinced to sell themselves on the streets for cash that they brought back to him, but in the sense that he was a "free spirit." Amazingly enough, he generally caught any woman he pursued even though most knew he was married, but open to meeting new women.

Those who shared forbidden time with Darius warned upcoming prospects about his ability to talk his way into their hearts and minds. Darius had what many call "The Gift of Gab," which in his case meant the uncanny ability to make a woman feel she was the best thing since sliced bread. The words that flowed from his mouth allowed a woman to let down her guard and get too comfortable in his presence. It could be the month of February, and Darius could actually convince a woman to take off her blouse because it was way too hot in the office. He also knew how to listen to a woman and convince her that what she was talking about was the most important thing in the world. But no matter how many "red flags" were thrown at Darius' prey, he always managed to get them to ignore the signs until it was too late. No matter how hard a woman tried to get Darius to leave his wife and commit to her, he always managed to thwart her efforts and remain married.

Darius' wife was a lovely young, beautiful black woman, named Monica. Together, they had two blessed children, Kayla and Chauncey. Monica was a college graduate and an executive assistant for a popular law firm in Harlem, New York. She was quite intelligent and knew how to make every dollar she earned work for her. Monica also knew how to triple her earnings in the stock market on an annual basis. Many men found Monica very attractive. She was classy with her beauty, though. She didn't wear too much makeup or dress provocatively. Most of the time, Monica was all about business. Many men flirted with her on the job, but she always maintained a serious persona that kept the hounds at bay.

Unfortunately, Monica knew all about the affairs her selfish husband was having. She really loved her family and would do anything to keep it together, so she developed a strong shell to cope with her husband's cheating habits and even embraced the motto, "Don't ask; don't tell." She completely withdrew herself, knowing that her husband needed professional help to deal with his infidelity. Nonetheless, the couple appeared very happy and blessed. Darius and his job title allowed them to own just about any car they desired, and Monica earned enough so they could afford their $600,000.00 colonial-style home in Scotch Plains, New Jersey.

The huge house was gorgeous. It came with four spacious custom bedrooms, three of which were 20' x 15', and the master bedroom was 23' x 18' with a full bath. Those who entered the house from the front door would find themselves in a spacious 25' x 20' living area. Beautiful furniture, complete with earth-tone, multicolored sofas, could be seen on mahogany-colored carpet throughout. There was even a large, flat-screen television on a glass entertainment center, where all of Darius's friends loved to watch sports. Exotic vases stood in three of the four corners of the room, giving it a Eurocentric appearance. The beige and white brick fireplace, with matching chimney, in the back of the room was absolutely astonishing to look at. Just above the fireplace was a bronze-framed mirror almost large enough to capture the image of the entire room. Its craftsmanship was second to none. The beautiful vanilla-colored drapes and curtains accented the furniture. Standing in the middle of the giant room, a person could go in one of four directions, including the spacious two-car garage and work area, complete with plenty of high-tech drills, saws, and other fancy tools.

The garage was admired by all who saw it. It was meticulously clean for a garage. Two large vehicles could park inside with no problem at all. The work area also had enough room for exercise equipment, complete with dumbbells, pull-up bars, and a bench press with free weights, located in the rear corner. Adjacent to the garage was a spacious 20' x 12' enclosed patio, complete with a beautiful furniture set. The patio was well insulated for occupancy anytime of the year. A unique ceiling fan, beige and trimmed in gold to match the sofas and coffee table, occupied the center of the ceiling. On the coffee table in the center of the room were neatly placed Jet, Black Enterprise, Ebony, ESPN and Sports Illustrated magazines. There was also a 42" flat-screen TV that displayed clear, high-quality digital programming. This is where the lady of the house and her girlfriends gathered to watch Lifetime, B.E.T. After Dark, and love stories.

A stairway in the living room led to ten steps carpeted with the same carpet that was in the living room. The steps led to a rather long hallway that sported a large mirror on one wall. The wallpaper was a thick and lustrous ivory white, trimmed in burgundy and bronze, silky to the touch. Anyone who saw it for the first time complimented Monica on the selection. Down the hallway, one child's bedroom was to the left, and the other to the right. One room was pink and the other blue, one for a boy and one for a girl. Further down the hallway was a full bath with a Jacuzzi tub/shower large enough for at least four people. The room was tiled with multi- colored earth tones---beige, light brown, and bone shades. The white throughout the room were trimmed in bronze, to match the bronze rug on the floor.

At the end of the hallway was the entrance to the spacious 22' x 20' master bedroom, complete with plush gold-trimmed burgundy carpet. The furniture was solid oak, and the bed sat on four pedal stools that raised the bed three feet from the floor. Laying in it was like floating on a huge lily pad down a slow-moving river. The curtains were a soft shade of rose to compliment the color scheme in the room. Mounted on one wall in front of the bed was a 52" flat-screen TV with the newest state-of-the-art technology. Large mirrors on the ceiling enabled some-one to get a full view of him- or herself while lying in the bed or on the floor, which was perfect for "visual stimulation" during any activity.

Outside, the home was beautifully landscaped with 8' tall spruce trees, giving the home a natural sense of privacy. Exotic flowers from Europe, in shades of blue, purple, pink, yellow and white, adorned the front yard. The backyard featured a huge in-ground swimming pool, with a medium-sized Jacuzzi attached to it. The water was a deep crys-tal blue. To the rear of the pool was a large Tikki bar that could host up to eight people. Needless to say, Darius and Monica lived well.

The day of the cookout, the temperature was a pleasant 85 degrees and practically no humidity. A slight breeze paid the area a visit just as it began to get too hot for those who were a little overdressed. The songbirds chirped in the blue sky, not a cloud in sight. The familiar smell of a barbecue permeated throughout the neighborhood as the charcoal-flavored meats cooked on the grill in the backyard. The sun was bright but not annoyingly beaming. Some would call it a perfect summer day. Great numbers of guests arrived and conversed among themselves, as R&B music played in the background. People were screaming and laughing with joy as they reunited with folks they hadn't seen in a while. Others were introduced to those they'd never met. At-traction was in the air; beautiful people were everywhere, and even the ones who were not as pleasing to the eye made up for it with their sparkling personality and style. Darius felt the need to formally intro-duce Isaac to a few select individuals. One of these folks was a fine, well-built sista by the name of Jasmine. When Isaac laid eyes on her and began to look her over, he was very impressed, especially with her pretty hazel eyes and her light almond skin. Isaac also admired the natural feminine curves that complemented her full-figured body. Jasmine had a smile that displayed her flawless pearly white teeth. Isaac was mesmerized by her voluptuous lips that set upon her exotic features. He almost melted when he observed Jasmine's long wavy hair, even though he wasn't sure whether it was natural or a weave.

"It is my utmost pleasure to introduce you to one of America's most eligible bachelors---Isaac!" said Darius. Isaac's heart began to beat just a little faster than normal, but he kept his composure and extended his hand to greet Jasmine. Isaac was displaying his most sincere GQ Smile, and Jasmine was thinking to herself, "Thank you Jesus; thank you Jesus; thank you Jesus!" Jasmine spotted Isaac when he made his grand entrance. She was so excited to meet this mysterious man. "Girl, keep it together!" she kept telling herself. She didn't want to give Isaac the impression that she was desperately looking for a man. But the most attractive thing about Isaac was the lack of a wedding ring on his finger.

Darius could sense the attraction between Isaac and Jasmine so, he decided to give the two some privacy. "I'll leave you two alone, so that you can get to know each other." As Darius walked away, Isaac and Jasmine looked at one another with a loss for words. Jasmine waited for Isaac to break the ice by striking up a conversation on the subject of his choice, while Isaac pondered how he would do this. Jasmine was far too classy for him to come at her like she was a Hood Rat or a lady with no self-respect. So, Isaac chose to be the perfect gentleman without being corny. "Jasmine is a pretty name," he said. "Woman, you are wearing the hell out of that body dress!" Jasmine began to blush and melt into Isaac's hands. She kept her cool because she didn't want to be too obvious.

"Thank you for the complement," said Jasmine. "And if you don't mind me saying so, you don't look half bad yourself!" Isaac could tell from her body language that Jasmine was digging him. She had a glowing smile on her pretty face. She gave Isaac full eye contact and her complete attention. Isaac began to take it a slight step further just to "seal the deal" of setting up a date with Jasmine. He gently, yet deliberately, grasped her left hand and as he caressed it, said, "A real man can tell a lot about a woman by examining her hands!" Jasmine knew that Isaac was flirting with her, but she didn't mind. In fact, she paid careful attention to him to try to observe whether he was a genuine gentleman or a player.

Isaac continued to look over Jasmine's hands, moist, yet not oily. He took special note of her well-manicured nails. He was particularly impressed with the unique, exquisite stripes of brown, beige, and white. Embedded in each nail was a set of four rhinestones in the shape of a diamond. Her nails perfectly matched her dress that caressed her body curves. "Jasmine, I can tell that you're a woman who takes good care of herself," Isaac said. "I would like to see you again so that you and I can get to know each other better. Would that be possible?" Before Jasmine could respond, Isaac raised her hand that he had been holding and slightly tilted his head downward, but not losing eye contact. Isaac planted a soft, yet firm, kiss on the back side of Jasmine's hand. "He is just too cute!" she thought. She agreed to go out with him again as they exchanged cell phone numbers. Wanting to put a cherry on top of the cake he'd just made, Isaac, whipped out his leather Roca Wear wallet and brandished one of his business cards from the non-profit association he worked for. Jasmine was impressed but worked hard at not showing it. She simply turned and walked away.

Isaac went to get something to eat and continued to enjoy the cookout. Darius and Monica knew how to throw a party. They had beef-barbecued spare ribs; grilled barbecued chicken; barbecued baked beans with ground hamburger meat; and fried seafood including whiting, Tilapia, shrimp, and scallops; baked macaroni and cheese; tossed salad, potato salad; dirty rice; collard greens and cabbage smothered in smoked turkey tails; southern fried chicken; fruit salad; chocolate cake; pineapple upside-down cake; peach cobbler; French vanilla sheet cake; and sweet potato pie. There was enough food to feed an army. To top it all off, Darius and Monica had the finest Spirits money can buy. Their guests had full access to a wonderful display of Cognac, Bacardi, E&J brandy, Crown Royale, Chivas Regal, and all kinds of assorted sweet and dry wines, as well as cases of Corona, Heineken, Samuel Adams, and Guinness Brewed beers. One had to be careful not to over indulge to avoid either getting a belly ache from eating too much or a DWI while trying to make it back home. After partying with Darius and his wife, Isaac was ready to retire for the evening. So, after saying goodbye to everyone at the party, he got into his luxury sports car and departed.

Chapter 2

Getting Down to Business

bout a week later, Darius called to see how Isaac enjoyed himself at the cookout, and to inquire whether he made any advances on Jasmine. "What's up man?" Isaac answered during a particularly dull moment at work. "You sure know how to put it down, my good sidekick! I really enjoyed myself at the cookout you put together last weekend!"

"Man, you must have been reading my mind because, I was just calling you to ask how you enjoyed yourself at the barbecue," Darius said. "Hey Isaac, I peeped you conversing with my wife's best girlfriend, Jasmine."

"Oh yeah, she is one fine specimen of a lady." answered Isaac.

"Are you seriously considering pursuing Jasmine?" asked Darius. "If so, I can let Monica know you're interested, and she could put in a good word for you"

"Yeah, that would be nice," answered Isaac. "Tell Monica any good information that will give me some cool points with her girl Jasmine would be greatly appreciated."

Darius was excited for Isaac. "Isaac, you are my main man and the whole nine yards, but I must keep it real with you!" Isaac paused momentarily to catch his breath because he was expecting Darius to tell him about some negative quality of Jasmine's. He was also hoping that Darius wasn't going to reveal some intimate relationship they had in the past because Isaac usually didn't get seriously involved with someone who had any previous attachments with his family or friends. He even developed a code: "Never put your nose where everyone else goes." "Isaac, I always had a secret crush on Jasmine," said Darius, "but I never pursued her because, I met her best friend, Monica, first. I always fantasized about what it would be like to hold Jasmine, man, what it would be like to kiss her full lips, and I don't just mean the ones on her face! "Isaac," continue Darius, "if you're lucky enough to put Jasmine in your stable, I want to know how the love making is before you guys become too serious."

Isaac was relieved that Darius had never made love to Jasmine. "Yeah, whatever, 'D,'" said Isaac. "Let's take one thing at a time. Hopefully your wife can give me an advantage with Jasmine with some words of inspiration on my behalf." Darius assured Isaac that once Monica told Jasmine about all of Isaac's good qualities, she'd think he walked on water. Darius also knew that Monica thought very highly of Isaac. "I'll call Jasmine sometime tomorrow," said Isaac, "so have Monica contact her before then."

"No problem Kat-Daddy," Darius replied. "Consider it done!" The two said their goodbyes and hung up.

The following evening, Isaac was home from another challenging day at the office. Raising funds and resources for the underprivileged in his community was hard work, but satisfying for Isaac. But now that his day was finished, it was time to dedicate some precious time to himself. So, he retired to his spacious living room where he exercised his well-developed body, jogging on the treadmill for 30 minutes at 8 mph, followed by push-ups, sit-ups, deep knee bends, pull-ups, and dips. This regular workout regiment allowed Isaac to stay physically fit naturally. The calisthenics let him work with his natural body weight, rather than piling on all exaggerated bulkiness that weight lifters accrue by tearing their muscles rather than working them. Isaac completed his workout with a giant cup of ice water to cool himself off. Then he walked over to the sofa, and stretched out to relax on it, and then pondered what to do with the rest of the night. As he looked at his watch, he noticed that the night was still young. So he popped a smooth Jazz CD into his Boise stereo system and played Najee, one of his favorite jazz artists. The relaxing sound of smooth jazz at the end of a hard day of work would release the greatest tension from even the most authoritarian State Corrections warden. Then, he lit a small candle and placed it under an oil-burning ornament, burning a unique musk fragrance that filled the room. Next, he picked up his cell phone and hit the speed dial button to contact Jasmine. The phone rang about five times, and then Isaac heard a sultry voice on the other end of the line. "Hello?" Isaac's heartbeat began to pick up speed. He knew it was Jasmine, and he was excited to hear her voice for the first time since the barbecue.

Not wanting to seem too eager, Isaac took a deep breath and sighed ever so gently with extreme control. Then he put on his smooth monotone voice and said, "Hello, stranger; it's been a long time since I heard from you! It's me, Isaac; we met at the cookout last weekend."

Jasmine was excited that Isaac was finally calling her. Her blood rushed to her heart and she developed goose bumps on her arms and the back of her neck. "Oh yeah, I remember you," Jasmine replied. "How have you been?"

"I've been fine," Isaac responded. "You know you've been on my mind lately, right?"

"What do you mean that I have been on your mind?" Jasmine said as she blushed on the other end of the phone.

"I don't want to come off too strong," Isaac replied, "but I'm very eager to have some quality one-on-one time with you to get to know you better."

Jasmine beamed a smile so wide that every tooth shone bright as she responded, "Well, I think I'd like to see you again, as well. You seemed like an interesting person when we first met."

Isaac was a fast thinker on his feet. He was very spontaneous in his conversation, and the way words flowed from his mouth made whomever he spoke to believe he was serious about the subject matter being discussed. "Well, since you find me interesting and the good Lord knows that I find you alluring," said Isaac, "when can I pick you up so that we can get better acquainted?"

Jasmine could hardly contain herself. "Look at you!" she said in her excited high-pitched voice. "You just know I'm going on a date with you, huh? You're just too confident with your game, aren't you?"

Isaac felt himself slipping into Mack-Mode as he extended and crossed his legs while folding his arms behind his head. "Oh no! I do not play games, Jasmine," Isaac replied. "I'm just serious about getting to know you better, Sweetie Pie. The moment you made it crystal clear that you were interested and wanted to get to know me better, I just got straight to the point to make that happen."

Isaac was saying all the right things without being cocky or arrogant. Little did he realize that Jasmine was already anxious and couldn't wait to meet Isaac all alone on an actual date. Isaac didn't want to draw out the conversation too long; he didn't want to bore her by talking too much. He wanted to leave a hint of mystery lingering over Jasmine's mind about how their first date would go. "Look here, Jasmine," Isaac explained, "I had a very long day at work, and I'm just turning in for the evening. I'm extremely excited to talk to you over the phone, and I'll look forward to communicating with you face to face. So, I'll pick you up on Friday night and have the night all planned out for us. Is that all right with you, Jasmine?"

Jasmine was astounded as well as aroused by Isaac's leadership and mysterious qualities. "Sure, that sounds real nice, but I haven't given you my address yet," said Jasmine. "And I don't know enough about you yet to relinquish my place of residence to a stranger," she said jokingly.

"Well, I can respect that," Isaac came back smoothly. "If it makes you feel any better, you can meet me at my place, and we can start our evening from here."

Jasmine felt as if he'd just said "checkmate." Every time she joked about not meeting with him, he just had to "countermove" to negate her attempt, until finally Isaac's quick-witted answers backed Jasmine in a corner. "That's cool," answered Jasmine. "Where do you live?"

Isaac gave her directions to his bachelor pad. "Jasmine, I look forward to seeing you once again," he said, as he ended the call. "This time it'll be just you and me." Isaac began to laugh in his low, deep voice. Jasmine found his laugh to be very sexy and devilish at the same time.

"Okay, I'll be there Friday night, eight o'clock sharp," said Jasmine. The two said good night for the evening.

Once Isaac hung up his phone, he stood up and began to dance as if he had a woman in his arms. He knew he left a lasting impression on Jasmine and that she was astonished with him. Meanwhile, Jasmine was in her apartment totally anxious for Friday to arrive so she could go on her date with Isaac. She took a shower to cool herself off from what she felt to be a hot conversation with a man that she was deeply attracted to. As the two lay in their separate homes and beds, they thought about all the possibilities that could happen when they got together. They both imagined would it would be like to experience being on top of each other during a steamy love-making session. Jasmine imagined how good it would feel to be embraced in Isaac's muscular arms and chest, and she wondered how good it would feel for Isaac to pick her up and carry her to the bed or couch and lay her on her back. Jasmine found herself pondering over Isaac kissing her passionately as the two rocked each other's world. Meanwhile, Isaac was relaxing on his bed fantasizing about Jasmine's soft cinnamon-butter skin on top of his body. He envisioned Jasmine's full set of lips grazing gently upon his most intimate spots, lightly licking and sucking on his neck, as she worked her way down. Needless to say, the two greatly anticipated meeting one another and enjoying each other's company. They were still trying to be realistic and professional, though. They kept telling themselves that it's only a date with someone they're merely attracted to physically, and that they really didn't know each other yet. But after a short while, the two fell asleep with one another on their minds.

Every couple of hours Isaac would wake up to use the bathroom or get a glass of ice water. Each time he daydreamed about how he planned to treat Jasmine on their first date and where he would take her. Isaac had it all planned out. He knew how he was going to approach Jasmine without coming off like a player or making himself look like a sucker. Isaac knew what kind of impression he wanted to leave Jasmine with. He didn't want to splurge on her or spoil her on the first date; he didn't want to buy her or give her the impression that he wanted to purchase her every desire. Isaac wanted her to respect him because of the way he treated her, not because of how deep his pockets appeared to be.

Isaac was well seasoned and experienced in the dating scene. He knew from personal experience that first impressions last a lifetime. His philosophy was to treat a woman with utmost respect while getting to know her. In Isaac's mind, a woman always deserved a certain level of respect to start with, and her actions would dictate any change in a man's attitude toward her. And while didn't believe a man had to spend astronomical amounts of money on a woman to demonstrate his affections, he also didn't believe a man should be frugal with his generosity in taking her on a date for the first time. A man had to be well balanced when dating a woman. Isaac knew that if he gave a woman too much, she would come to expect marvelous things from him all the time. On the other hand, if he didn't give her enough, she would lose interest altogether. Bearing all this in mind, Isaac formulated what he felt to be a solid game plan for Jasmine and their first evening alone together.

Chapter 3

The Rendezvous

riday evening arrived quickly. Isaac was just finalizing his proposal for a management plan to open an after-school program for not-so-fortunate children, which included counseling, sports and big brother/sister programs. He received great satisfaction for putting in an honest day of hard work. His mission was to do at least one positive thing every month to make a difference in his community. Isaac took his job seriously. He was very professional in carrying out his daily duties and hardly ever took a break until each assigned task was completed. He was very creative in formulating plans and new ideas to generate opportunities for inner-city children. Isaac had a great desire to make a positive difference in lives of anyone who needed help. He believed that since children didn't ask to be born into this world, it was their parents' job to provide for them. If they didn't, the programs he developed would ensure that any child got a fair chance to succeed. But he also didn't believe in handouts simply because a person needed something. His philosophy was to help those who were making an honest effort to help themselves. And now that he'd accomplished that mission for the day, he was now completely focused on his first date with Jasmine.

Jasmine was an accountant for Price Waterhouse of New York. She had also just completed a demanding day of work. Like Isaac, Jasmine also took her job seriously, barely taking any breaks until she completed what was expected of her. She handled her abundant workload with great tenacity and meticulousness and rarely made any mistakes. In fact, she had one of the highest accuracy ratings in the company and developed a marketable reputation in her field. Jasmine was a hustler on the grind, determined to be one of the best accountants in her company, while also studying tenaciously for her CPA. Jasmine was extremely focused when it came to performing her duties. During her leisure time she went to the local gym three to four times a week to exercise her well-toned physique. Her workout regiment consisted of 45 minutes of aerobic training, light weights, and occasional swimming. Jasmine also maintained good eating habits throughout the week, but on the weekends she splurged on small amounts of junk foods to keep her sane. She knew if she ate healthy all year around, she would eventually find eating miserable and boring. Jasmine was big-boned, but she was thick and toned in all the right spots. At 4:30, it was time to leave work and go home to get ready for her date. She was a little fatigued but, when she thought of driving to Isaac's place to spend the evening with him, her adrenaline kicked into high gear. So, she rushed home to prepare for her much-anticipated night with Isaac.

Meanwhile, Isaac made it home through the rough New Jersey Turnpike traffic. He entered his bachelor pad with a step of excitement and confidence, certain that his planned evening for Jasmine would be most impressive. Isaac walked briskly across his living room right into the master bedroom. As he stepped, one piece of clothing came off his body with each step, as if spirits were helping him undress. Isaac was a smooth operator who moved fluidly, but deliberately. Isaac was very particular about how he prepared for any event. First he rinsed his mouth out with mouthwash, and brushed and flossed his teeth. Then he turned on some steaming hot water and splashed his cheeks and chin. Next he lathered his face with shaving cream to give himself a crisp shave and a flawlessly trimmed mustache. Then he entered the shower and gave himself an ultra clean washing from head to toe. After drying off, Isaac oiled his body down in some homemade fragrant oils he concocted to give him a wonderful, yet unique, aroma. To complete his appearance for the evening, Isaac dressed himself in a fine navy blue and ivory pinstriped Brooks Brothers suit, California style---no tie and his ivory dress shirt unbuttoned at the top---revealing his masculine chest and diamond cross necklace. He completed his outfit with burgundy snake-skinned shoes and a black dress hat with a multicolored feather on one side. Isaac looked perfect in his full-body mirror; he managed to strike a balance. He didn't look like a playboy out to capture the attention of women everywhere, and he didn't look like a fruit loop of a nerd. Those who regularly saw Isaac's appearance classified him as a man with lots of class in a sexy sort of way.

As Isaac waited for Jasmine to arrive at his home, his telephone began to ring. "Hello," he answered. Darius was on the other end of the line. "Are you ready for tonight, my good brotha?" he asked anxiously. "I was eaves dropping on Monica's conversation with Jasmine the other night. She was giving you a bunch of props, man. If I didn't know any better, I would have thought Monica wanted you for herself!" There was a slight pause over the line for a moment. Then Darius laughed and said, "Well anyway, with all the compliments that Monica gave to Jasmine, there's no doubt in my mind that you're off to a good start. All you have to do is capitalize off the foundation she laid for you."

"Good looking out for me, Big D." said Isaac.

"No problem at all, man," Darius replied. "Just remember, you have to give me all the juicy details about you and Jasmine, especially if it ends in a night of hot passion." Isaac assured him that he would let him know what happened on this anticipated evening. After all, Darius and Isaac had been good friends for many years and shared intimate details of their lives with one another, whether it was about sex, family, or helping each other prepare for upcoming college exams.

As the two concluded the phone call, Darius reflected on Monica's conversation with Jasmine the night before. He was uncomfortable about Monica bragging about his good friend, Isaac. Darius remembered the words and lustful tone of voice of his dear wife Monica as she talked about Isaac. Monica was wearing a seductive red two-piece bikini set as she lay in bed talking to Jasmine. "Girl, you are a blessed woman to have a date with Isaac this weekend!" she told Jasmine. "I have known Isaac for a long time. He's been close friends with Darius ever since I've known him. He always had his act together, girl," she continued. "He has a Bachelor of Arts degree and a job that pays well. And he is so fine---always was built like a Mandingo!" Monica's sultry tone of voice as she talked about Isaac infuriated him. He couldn't stand the thought of his wife being physically attracted to his main man. He didn't want Monica to know he was eaves dropping on their conversation, so he left the shower running so that Monica would think he was getting cleaned up. Deep down in Darius's heart, he knew that after listening to Monica, she was deeply attracted to him.

It was 7 p.m. Jasmine had just finished soaking in a warm bubble bath to relax for the evening to come. After she got out of the tub, she rubbed her curvy body down with Victoria Secret's fine lotion and smelled absolutely edible. Her hair was combed flawlessly as it lay across her shoulders and upper back. Jasmine beamed with natural beauty. All she needed was a light coat of lip gloss and eyeliner to highlight her glorious features. Now, she had to figure out which outfit to drape over her body. She didn't want to give the impression that she was eager to sleep with him on their first date. On the other hand, she didn't want to look like she was ready for church. Jasmine believed there had to be a balance of self-respect and sexiness. So, she elected to wear knee high-boots with ivory stockings and a black sport-cut skirt. Even though her skirt was by no means slutty, it hugged her body like a leather driving glove over a race car driver's hand, and revealed just enough to keep any admirer wondering how she would look without anything on. She topped off the alluring, but tasteful, ensemble with a pair of exotic white gold diamond hoop earrings and a matching diamond necklace. Needless to say, she looked and smelled good. She grabbed Isaac's address off the kitchen table and programmed it into her portable GPS. Then she grabbed her authentic black Coach bag, climbed into her full-bodied luxury Lexus sedan, and off she went.

The evening was particularly pleasant. The temperature was about 78 degrees with a very gentle breeze. The sky was clear and the sun had just begun to set. The city lights were just coming on. Traffic was active enough to keep Jasmine alert as she drove, but not so crowded that she'd end up frustrated before she ever reached her destination. Jasmine slid her Earth, Wind, and Fire CD into her car stereo, preparing to enter "relaxation mode." As she cruised the streets with grace, eager to see Isaac, she concentrated on not being too excited. After all, she didn't want Isaac to become overly confident in his approach. On her way to Isaac's Jasmine made a quick stop at a convenient store to pick up some mint chewing gum in case she and Isaac did decide to kiss each other later on. She remembered that she'd eaten blue onions in her grilled chicken salad earlier in the day and didn't want to get caught off guard with bad breath. When it came to foul odor, blue onions could put their white counterparts to shame, but she felt the gum would effectively ward off any funky fumes that might flow out of her mouth while talking or kissing.

Jasmine located Isaac's home with ease, thanks to her GPS in the windshield. Excitedly, she pulled in front of his home, feeling like a child on Christmas morning. She arrived right on time, not too early and not too late, which allowed Isaac to wait with anticipation without becoming overly frustrated. Jasmine sat in the car for a minute after she arrived and let it idle for a bit longer. She wanted to get her full bearings now that she'd arrived. She gave herself one final look-over in the mirror. "OK, girl," she said to herself, "lights, camera, action. It's show time; let's keep it together." After psyching herself up with this little phrase, she knew she was ready for her big night.

saac heard Jasmine pull up along the curb. He was as excited as she was. He too rushed to give himself a final look-over in the mirror, and was pleased at his reflection. Then he walked smoothly toward the front door to greet Jasmine. As he strolled down the hallway full of confidence, he could hear the heels of his dress shoes clicking like a professional tap-dancer on stage. Walking with a high level of swagger, excited at Jasmine's arrival, he took deep, controlled breaths before opening the door. He didn't want Jasmine to see him sweat like a rookie. After all, he was a seasoned dating veteran, and now it was show time---time to impress Jasmine with his suave demeanor and charming ways. He knew how to win a lady's heart---by treating her like a lady without appearing phony. Isaac was a gentleman at heart, but he knew that every now and then he let his wild side take over.

Jasmine exited her car like a panther in the night, shutting the door behind her and setting her car alarm. As she moved seductively as she strolled up Isaac's walkway toward the front door, expecting that this date would be something wonderful to remember, she was quite impressed at the meticulous landscaping. The grass was particularly green, and exotic bushes and flowers surrounded his front porch and garage. Jasmine was also impressed with the long driveway and how it curved upward to his two-car garage. And once she feasted her eyes on his midnight black Aston Martin sports car in the driveway with custom tags saying, "BLESSED," she knew he did quite well for himself. The fact that Monica had already told her that only made Jasmine pay close attention to confirm her statement. Jasmine arrived at the front door and rang the doorbell.

Isaac was already admiring Jasmine through the peep hole on the other side of the door. He didn't want to appear too anxious, so he waited for 20 seconds before opening it. As Isaac opened the door, he smiled his most charming smile and said, "Hello, Jasmine. My goodness, you look so nice this evening!" Jasmine began to blush as she stepped inside Isaac's place, once again impressed by how he lived and how clean the house was. A unique aroma permeated the home, but she couldn't quite identify the fragrance. Nonetheless, it was most soothing to her nose. "Let me show you around the house," Isaac said. "I hope you like it."

Isaac guided her to each of his three bedrooms. The first was a guest room. The wallpaper was beige with white trim; the floor was covered with dark gold carpet, with matching curtains on the windows. The queen-sized bed sported a gold and beige comforter set to match the color scheme of the room. The second room was his office. It had deep brown Pergo-style floors and a matching queen-sized wooden sleigh bed. The curtains were ivory, complimenting the bed and floor. An oval-shaped rug lay in the center of the floor next to an entertainment center, and a state-of-the-art computer sat on the desktop. In one corner of the room was a high-gloss oak shelf with two different sets of encyclopedias sitting on it. Jasmine paid close attention to the art that was hanging on the walls---monumental paintings of people who changed to world---Martin Luther King, Jr., Mohammed Ali, Jackie Robinson, Rosa Parks and W.E.B. Dubois. Each painting was framed in oak-finished frames. The paintings really filled the room with a sense of pride.

Next, Isaac showed Jasmine the master bedroom. Relatively larger than the previous rooms, this room had a king-sized bed with black satin sheets, black-and-white striped pillow cases, and a pine finished floor. Even though the comforter was folded in half, one could admire the zebra design. The dressers and entertainment center shone a high-gloss black finish, trimmed in bronze. The master bath was decorated in shades of neutral colors, contrasting his bedroom colors nicely. The tile was the color of cracked wheat and the shower stall was quite deep. Jasmine was most impressed with the roomy closets in each bedroom. She was the typical woman, admiring a closet that would hold a hundred pairs of shoes and thousands of outfits that only get worn seasonally.

Next, Isaac showed her the spacious eat-in kitchen. The table was large enough to seat six people easily on any occasion. The light brown cabinets were relatively new. The tile floor was a beautiful shade of slate gray. A ceiling fan in the center complimented the color of the table. Then they walked into the laundry room, painted in a particularly inviting shade of vanilla. Jasmine was impressed by the fresh smell of fabric softener throughout the room. She appreciated the large state-of-the-art washer and matching dryer. By this time, Jasmine sincerely appreciated Isaac's taste in fashion and design.

As they proceeded to the hall bath, Jasmine was bedazzled by the extra large Jacuzzi hot tub and the elegant brown and white tile, with matching towel sets hanging from the towel ring. The light beige curtains were trimmed in glossy white. The living room was spacious with beautiful hard wood floors. The plush oatmeal-colored sofa and matching loveseat could easily seat six people. The reclining chair in the corner of the room made the set complete. There was a huge flat-screen TV mounted on the wall and a bear rug in the middle of the floor; its almond fur blended well with the floor. Alongside the classic rug was an antique marble coffee table with swirls of beige and white accenting its boundaries. Four little angels acted as the legs of the table, their wings arching upward to hold the clear, crystal table top in perfect position. Next, Isaac showed Jasmine the spacious dining room next to the living room. Inside was a large high-gloss oak table with chairs to match, enough room for 8 people. Two 7-foot high-quality wood cabinets stood across the room. On the shelves of one cabinet were antique dishes, potter dolls, and vases. On the other were fine desserts: pound cakes, lemon cakes, sweet-potato pies, and tarts.

The finished basement, which was as large as the entire home, was the best part of the tour. Once Jasmine walked downstairs, she was impressed with the attractive designer flooring, illuminated in light beige. The light beige walls throughout matched the floor nicely. A 54" plasma TV sat in on corner, and to the right was a row of at least 300 DVD movies in alphabetical order. In another corner was a wood bar, color coordinated to match the wood floor. The bar was fully loaded with Jim Bean whiskey, Hennessey Cognac, Grey Goose Vodka, assorted Brandy, Captain Morgan Spiced Rum, Johnny Walker Black Label Scotch Whiskey Blend, Crown Royal Canadian Whiskey, and much more. Next to the bar was a 6' wine cabinet that held at least 30 bottles of corked fine wine. In the middle of the basement was a large cherry wood pool table with a camel suede cover. Expensive Egyptian paintings, beautifully framed in gold with a hint of burgundy, hung on most of the walls. A huge entertainment center sat next to the wine cabinet that had a state-of-the-art stereo system with large speakers. There was a living area on the other side of the basement, complete with a plush, cream-colored Lazy Boy style sofa, and matching loveseat and lounge chairs. Jasmine was particularly captivated by the colorful flashing lights, chrome legs, and onyx frame of the large pinball machine on the side of one of sofa. She also took note of the Lord's Supper hanging on one wall, which let her appreciate Isaac's spiritual side. As Isaac showed Jasmine around the basement, he explained what each item meant to him, not trying to be boastful or arrogant; he merely had a story for everything in his home. She enjoyed listening to his words. Isaac opened a door in another corner of the house to reveal another spacious bathroom. Jasmine appreciated the wonderful craftsmanship of the shower stall and the carving of the tiles, all color coordinated in beige, bone, and eggshell white. As Isaac told her how he chose the colors, he occasionally slipped in a mild joke to make Jasmine laugh. Isaac was a real gentleman; he never made any distasteful advances, and Jasmine's mind was at great peace. "This brotha' has got it going on," she said to herself. "But I can't get too excited and let him know he is blowing my mind. Then it might go to his head, and he'll think he is all that!"

"Now that you've seen how I live, are you ready to enjoy yourself this evening?" he asked, as he finished showing Jasmine around.

"Yes, let's go!" she said in delight.

Isaac guided Jasmine to his car and opened the passenger side door for her. Then he got in on the driver's side. As he walked around to get into the car, Jasmine watched his stride and appreciated his clothing. "That man is sharp---look at those broad shoulders!" she said to herself. She was in absolute awe of Isaac's entire makeup. As he eased into the driver's seat, she smelled the unique, pleasant masculine aroma he concocted earlier. The smell filled the air inside the car, and Jasmine began to blush as she complimented him on how well he smelled that night. "Isaac, whatever oil or cologne you have on smells so good to me!" she said.

"Thank you," he said, a little more confident and comfortable now. He leaned toward her and inhaled deeply. "You don't smell too bad yourself!" he said. "What's that fragrance you're wearing this evening?"

Jasmine blushed and replied, "Oh I can't remember the name of it. I think it's a selection from Lady Fendi Perfumes."

Isaac put the key in the ignition and drove off into the early evening. The street lights were on, the sun hadn't fully set, and a slight breeze filled the air. They couldn't have asked for a more pleasant evening. Isaac put on an Isley Brother CD. "In between the Sheets" began to set the mood. Jasmine was impressed by his classical music selection and made Isaac seem mature for his age. She halfway expected Gangsta Rap, which would not have been her choice for music on a date. Isaac turned the music down so that the two of them could hear each other talk. "Jasmine, I have been thinking about where a woman of your beauty would like to go on a first date," Isaac said, smiling. "I just hope you enjoy the evening that I have carefully planned for you." Jasmine told Isaac to relax and that she would appreciate where ever he took her. A serious deep rumble could be heard from the stainless steel mufflers due to the 400 hp engine. The two cruised the streets without a care in the world.

Moments later, Isaac pulled into the parking lot of a jazz night club/restaurant called "The Zodiac." After Isaac exited his vehicle, he opened the door for Jasmine. Then he extended his bent arm for Jasmine to rest her hand on to be escorted inside. "Do you have a reservation?" the hostess asked as they entered The Zodiac.

"Yes I do," Isaac answered confidently. "The name is Isaac, and I have a party of two."

"Ah yes, here you are," replied the hostess, as she looked at her reservation list sitting on the podium. "Right this way, Sir; your table for two is ready." Jasmine was impressed that Isaac took time to make reservations on such a busy Friday night. The lighting inside the club was slightly dim but not to the point where they had to squint to focus. A disco ball rotated colors around the room from the ceiling. As Jasmine and Isaac were escorted to their table, they both took note of the solid glass floors, which revealed an array of bright orange, red, and white fish underneath. "Those are beautiful fish," Jasmine said excitedly. "What kind are they?"

"I have no idea," the hostess replied. "But I'd imagine they're tropical."

"They're called Koi, and they're from Japan," Isaac interjected. Jasmine was once again impressed with Isaac's mentality. He seemed very well educated, intelligent in a cool sort of way, not nerdy like most educated people.

As Isaac and Jasmine arrived at their seats, they noticed the beautiful beige marble table and multicolored Earth-tone leather seats that complimented the atmosphere.

Before Jasmine could sit down, Isaac said, "Allow me the honor of taking your jacket and getting your seat."

"I could get use to this type of treatment," Jasmine thought as she blushed. Isaac smoothly slid Jasmine's lightweight jacket off of her curvy torso and hung it on the pillar belonging to their table. He then eased Jasmine's chair out just enough for her to fit in between the chair and the table. "Thank you very much Mr. Isaac," Jasmine said as she sat down. "You're such a gentleman tonight."

"What do you mean 'tonight?'" Isaac replied. "Oh I see; you got jokes this evening." The two of them began to laugh at each other's playful sarcasm. As Isaac and Jasmine looked over the menu to decide what to order for dinner, a live band began playing wonderful Jazz music. The rhythm filled the air and gave the atmosphere a seductive and calm aura.

"Is that Kenny G the band is playing?" Jasmine asked.

"Oh yeah, that's my man," Isaac replied. "And the band is no joke." The music really broke the ice between the two since they both enjoyed the same music. Isaac was relieved that Jasmine was enjoying his restaurant selection and choice of events that evening. At the same time, Jasmine was thinking that she'd finally met a man with some class and good taste.

Isaac and Jasmine's waitress came over to their table. "Hello, my name is Cynthia. Welcome to The Zodiac this evening. I will be serving you tonight. Could I start you guys off with some drinks?" Cynthia asked.

"Yes, I would like to order for both of us, if Jasmine doesn't mind," Isaac replied.

Jasmine raised her eye brows in astonishment. "Wow, a man that is not afraid to take charge. This is too good to be true!" she thought.

"Sure, you can order for both of us," said Jasmine. "But I hope you have good taste in food because you don't even know me yet. How do you know what I like to eat and drink?"

"Trust me Jasmine," Isaac responded confidently. "I'll only order the finest food and drinks for you, and if you don't approve, I'll send it back and let you order for yourself. I only ask that you allow me the opportunity to turn you on to something that you may not have encountered? Does that sound fair?"

"Sure," Jasmine said. "That's fine. Maybe you can introduce me to something tasty and delicious," she said with a devilish look on her face. Isaac knew Jasmine was flirting with him; he had her just where he wanted her. He knew that when Jasmine asked him to introduce her to something tasty and delicious, she wasn't talking about the menu. He knew she was highly interested by the way she smiled and looked directly into his eyes. Isaac asked the waitress to give him a few moments to decide what he wanted to order. The waitress walked away to tend to the many other customers there that night.

After examining the menu for several minutes Isaac said, "I'll start us off with some drinks." He raised his hand to get Cynthia's attention. She walked over to their table with her white pad in hand and asked, "I see you've decided?"

"Oh yes," Isaac responded. "We'd like to start out with Malibu pineapple rum mixed with orange juice and a splash of cran-raspberry juice on the rocks."

"Sounds like a good mix," Cynthia said. "I'll have to try that myself sometime."

"Yeah, you look like the type who knows which type of drink mix can get a woman to relax and do anything you want," Jasmine said.

Isaac began smiling as he said in a modest tone of voice, "Oh no, I would never get a woman drunk just so I can take advantage of her. I believe they have a law against that. It's called date rape." Jasmine began to giggle because she could hear the sarcasm in his voice and noticed the indifferent expression on Isaac's face. "If I have to get a woman drunk to become intimate with me," Isaac continued, "then I need to let her go all together."

"That's right!" Jasmine agreed. "A lot of women fall prey to that kind of thing. They go on a date with a man they barely know and get too comfortable. So, they have a few drinks out of a false sense of security, and before they know it, they're at the man's disposal."

Isaac shook his head in approval. "At that point she can only hope that her date only has good intentions toward her," he said. "This con-artist world can be really dangerous. That's why you're lucky that you're with me and that my intentions are all good when it comes to you. Well, not all good, but even the not-so-good intentions are naughty in a good way."

Jasmine laughed and thought Isaac's comments were cute. While the two were conversing, Cynthia was busy eaves dropping and gaining interest in their table. Isaac was so busy flirting with Jasmine that he almost forgot Cynthia was still waiting for him to finish the drink order. His eyes opened wide in surprise, as he said, "Oh, I'm sorry for holding you up. You can get the drinks for now, and when you come back, I'll have decided what we're going to eat."

Cynthia smiled. "No problem, Mr. Friendly," she joked. "Since your intentions are so good, I'll ask that your drinks be made strong so that you can concentrate on the way you intend to make your date feel special." Isaac knew that the waitress was being sarcastic, but he didn't mind because Cynthia made him feel interesting enough for her to interject. Jasmine, on the other hand, thought that Cynthia was rude for listening in and even ignorant to confirm it with her shrewd comments.

"Wow," Isaac said. "I didn't realize this place required its waitresses to be comedians. You're so funny that I really have to take my hat off to you." Isaac was being playfully sarcastic, smiling ear to ear as he spoke to her. Cynthia laughed once again and said, "OK, I'll be back with your drinks."

s Cynthia walked away to get their drinks, she began purposely walking sexy to get Isaac's attention. Isaac turned his head slightly, but not to make it obvious to Jasmine that he was sneaking a peak at the waitress. Cynthia was an attractive lady. Isaac admired her beautiful light skin, long silky black hair, curvy torso, small waistline, tight voluptuous rump, and muscular calves. Cynthia looked back to see if Isaac was checking her out, and to her pleasure, he was. "Oh yeah, he's watching me," she thought. "And he likes what he sees." Cynthia knew Isaac wasn't married because while she was taking their drink order, to her delight, she noticed he wasn't wearing a wedding band. As far as she was concerned, Isaac was still fair game if Jasmine didn't fit the bill.

Isaac concentrated as best as he could not to let Jasmine see his lustrous gaze at Cynthia. So, he kept his head straight toward Jasmine yet, slightly tilted downward as if he were examining the menu. But when Isaac canted his eyes sharply in Cynthia's direction to admire her thick, curvy physique, Jasmine caught the direction of his lustful stare. "Oh no he didn't!" she thought to herself. "That's all right. He's a man, and that's what men do." Isaac didn't realize Jasmine saw him and lost some points in her book as a result. He attempted to play it off by ordering two of the largest lobsters available for the two of them once Cynthia returned, along with scallops, shrimp, baked potatoes, stuffed mushrooms, and two more drinks to top off his expensive order. Now, maybe the mood will lighten up, and Jasmine won't be thinking about Isaac drooling over Cynthia. After all, Isaac was there with Jasmine and his goal all week has been to impress her.

Jasmine was impressed with Isaac's fine, expensive taste, even though she was still uneasy and offended that Isaac was checking out their waitress. Cynthia was also impressed with Isaac's selection, although she didn't notice the more expensive items he ordered. Cynthia was only interested in keeping his attention on her instead of Jasmine. She began walking away extra seductively because she knew Isaac was looking her way. But Isaac caught himself this time and realized he may have been staring too deeply at his waitress in front of Jasmine once again. "So Jasmine, tell me a little more about yourself," he said to take his mind off of Cynthia.

"Well now let's see," thought Jasmine. "I have a very demanding career. As you already know, I'm an accountant, and my job is to be very observant of anything out of the ordinary when it comes to numbers. And I've become quite good at it. I do the same with people. My clients have different personalities, and it is my job to know what is on their minds and give them advice on how to maximize their gains and minimize any losses. For instance, I couldn't help but notice how you were staring at our waitress as if you were undressing her with your eyes. Let me give you some advice on that. If you continue to show more interest in the waitress, you will maximize your losses in losing my interest in you and minimize your gains in picking up the tramp. Either way it is a bad business move if you catch my drift." Isaac almost gagged on the glass of water he'd been sipping on, but he thought it was cute that Jasmine was showing her jealous and protective side.

"What are you talking about, sweetheart?" he said, attempting to play innocent. "I wasn't looking at Cynthia in that way; I was just admiring her dress."

Jasmine started laughing at Isaac's pitiful attempt at innocence. "You have to be kidding me, right?" she asked. "You expect me to believe that you were admiring her dress?"

Isaac knew his response was corny, but he didn't want to seem like a compulsive liar. "Look," he began. "I'm sorry for taking too long of a peek at the waitress, but we're here for you! My focus is on you, Jasmine, and I didn't mean to disrespect you in any way. So, let's not cry over spilled milk or make a big deal out of nothing. You and I came here together, and we will leave here together."

Jasmine started to smile because she knew Isaac was sincere about what he was saying. Sure he lost some points, but, his charm kept his head above water. Isaac was fast on his feet when it came to excuses, and this one kept him in the ball game. Jasmine was still eager to learn more about Isaac, something her body language also conveyed. Isaac was a great judge of character and he knew he was back in the driver's seat. He began to relax now that he thought the ice was broken. From this point on, he gave Jasmine full eye contact and nodded his head in approval of her every comment. Isaac knew he was slowly winning kudos. Like most women, Jasmine loved to talk and was delighted that Isaac appeared to take great interest in her conversation.

Before long, Cynthia returned with their food. Cynthia was still in her professional yet, seductive, mode, leaning over to reveal her cleavage as she placed the food on the table, plate by plate, far enough that Isaac could smell her Chanel for Women perfume. Isaac used his peripheral vision to gaze upon Cynthia's skin. He admired her almond complexion and sweet aroma that permeated from her chest and neck. Isaac smiled at Cynthia in a polite, professional manner as he thanked her for serving their meal. Jasmine paid close attention to Isaac's body language and tone of voice as he addressed Cynthia, even though she missed the free peep show. Cynthia knew how to flirt, but she made sure her gestures toward Isaac were in good taste and not deliberately disrespectful to Jasmine. Jasmine took note of the gestures but couldn't say anything to correct Cynthia for being disrespectful. "Enjoy your meal," said Cynthia as she walked away seductively. Isaac made sure he didn't watch her this time. He stiffened his neck tightly in Jasmine's direction, locked his eyes on her face, and smiled as if she were the only woman in the restaurant. Not wanting to appear jealous, Jasmine simply looked down at the food Cynthia placed in front of them.

Isaac could see that Cynthia made Jasmine feel uncomfortable. So, he immediately changed Jasmine's entire mood: "Let's pray before we indulge in our blessed meal," he said.

Once again, Jasmine was taken by surprise at this religious side Isaac displayed. "OK, that will be nice," she said as she smiled, revealing her beautiful white teeth.

They bowed their heads to go to their Heavenly Father in prayer. "Dear Lord in Heaven," began Isaac, "We come to you today to say 'thank you' for allowing us to meet each other and make it to this wonderful restaurant safely. We thank you for the wonderful meal that we are about to receive, Heavenly Father. And dear God, we just ask you to bless the hands that prepared this meal and allow this food to bring nourishment to our bodies. For all these blessings, we give thanks in Jesus name--- Amen."

Jasmine opened her eyes sporting a huge smile across her face. "Wow! This man never ceases to amaze me," she thought. "He is actually a God-fearing man!" And Jasmine was a God-fearing woman. In fact, she complimented Isaac on his choice of words to bless their splendid meal: "I had no idea that a smooth pimp like you had a personal relationship with God," she said.

"First of all, Miss Lady, I am not a pimp," Isaac replied. "Secondly, I do have a very personal relationship with the man upstairs. I am by no means perfect and may even fall to some of the temptations of this world, but I still am a child of God." Isaac smiled at Jasmine to reassure her that he was un-offended by her glib remark. He just kept the record straight in a professional manner to bring to light that people here on Earth are mortals who make plenty of mistakes. Isaac knew that Jasmine caught him gawking at the beautiful waitress and developed an indifferent opinion about his wandering eyes. He made it clear that just because he finds other women attractive, that doesn't mean that he's a pimp, player, or a lover boy. Isaac also knew that he should be more disciplined in keeping his eyes strictly on Jasmine while he was out with her. Once again, Isaac changed their thoughts from religion to the wonderful meal before them. "Look at this food. Doesn't it look good?" he asked. Jasmine agreed delightfully as she dug her fork into her collard greens smothered in smoked turkey tails. Isaac dug his fork into his cheesy baked macaroni and cheese. "Ooohhhs," "ahhhhs," and ummmms" resonated from their table.

Several moments later, the two had cleaned their plates completely. As the two sat back in their chairs to allow some space for their full bellies to expand, they smiled at each other. As Jasmine lay back in her chair, her stomach began to churn and bubble. She knew she'd consumed her food entirely too quickly and was going to pay the price for it. Her stomach began to ache sharply, and a rush of gas made a dash toward her torso in an attempt to escape her body. Jasmine didn't want to be embarrassed on her first date with Isaac, so, she clinched her thighs together and locked her sphincter muscle to prevent the inevitable from happening. It took all of Jasmine's energy to prevent the gas from creating the humiliating noise that should only be heard in a restroom. She succeeded in her strenuous attempt to entrap the gas that was determined to get out of her body. As a result, Jasmine's stomach made a whining noise like a cat in freezing water. Isaac heard the funny sound come from Jasmine's stomach, and he could determine from her stiffened cheeks that she was resisting her natural gas to exit her body. Isaac smoothly acted as if he didn't even notice Jasmine squirming like a snail that just had salt poured on it. The gas immediately passed toward the other exit of Jasmine's body, and she couldn't thwart off the ricochet that she originally created. The gas bounced off of her sphincter muscle and shot out of her mouth, releasing a thunderous burp. It was so deafening, it could be clearly heard by at least four tables of customers. The men just ignored Jasmine's natural release of gas, but her female counterparts looked at her in disgust. If looks could kill, Jasmine would have stopped breathing on the spot from all the scowls at her. Most men didn't even realize it was Jasmine who committed the offense. They didn't even bother to turn their heads because they thought it was the 300-pound man in the corner. Jasmine observed the women in the restaurant scowling at her in displeasure. She tried to play it off by shifting the blame to Isaac: "Dag, Isaac, excuse yourself," she said. "I warned you about embarrassing me in public." Isaac's eyes opened wide and his jaw dropped into his lap, shocked that Jasmine insinuated that it was he who belched like a gorilla.

"Well I did disrespect her by checking out the waitress," thought Isaac quickly, "so, I will take this one on the chin to even the score board." Isaac smiled reluctantly and replied aloud so everyone around them could hear: "Oh sure, honey, I'm sorry for burping like that. It's just that the food is so good here, and that burp got away from me." Jasmine put her head down and began to muffle her laughter so that it looked like she was ashamed of Isaac. She was a good actress.

At that moment, Cynthia came back to their table to see if they wanted coffee or desert. Both Jasmine and Isaac were too stuffed with the main course to eat anything else. Isaac asked for the bill so that he and Jasmine could return to his bachelor pad and continue getting to know each other better with fewer distractions. Isaac focused on Jasmine's pretty eyes to show the waitress he was there with Jasmine and had no intentions of flirting with her. He was not going to disrespect Jasmine by paying attention to the sexy waitress or anyone else. Cynthia picked up on the cold shoulder loud and clear, and put on her professional demeanor. She stood erect like a soldier would when addressing a superior and spoke to Isaac seriously and directly. "Sure thing," Cynthia said. "I'll be back with your bill in a moment."

"Hey, after this," Isaac said to Jasmine, "let's go back to my place to get better acquainted."

Jasmine was grinning with her left upper lip canted sharply in the air, as if to say "I don't know, man."

"I just think it would be better if we went back to my place to give us some privacy," Isaac reassured. "This restaurant has good food, but the atmosphere is not exclusive enough for us to really get to know each other. The place is getting crowded, and customers are talking and laughing loudly, and the moment I turn my head away from you, it looks as if I'm interested in another woman. Yeah, I see the expression on your face when the waitress is at our table. I like that, though. You have a jealous side that you can't hold back as much as you want to."

Jasmine respected Isaac's statement even though she knew it was part of his Mack-Game. "All right," she said. "I'll go with you to your home, so we kick it and get to know each other better."

Cynthia returned with their bill. Isaac pulled out his credit card to pay. Still in her professional mode, Cynthia accepted the card and went to the cash register to complete the transaction. Things seemed to be going better for Isaac and Jasmine now that the waitress had stopped throwing herself at Isaac. "Here is your credit card," Cynthia said when she returned to the table. "Please sign this receipt." Isaac complied and signed the appropriate copy. "OK, thank you," Cynthia said. "Here is your copy." Cynthia handed Isaac his receipt folded neatly in three folds, covering it completely with her own hand as she placed it in Isaac's hand. Isaac thanked her and put the copy in his pants pocket as he tipped Cynthia $40 for her service. Cynthia smiled from ear to ear because most of her customers barely leave her a 2 percent tip. As Isaac helped Jasmine with her jacket, he observed Cynthia cut her eye at him while Jasmine's back was to them. With a devilish smile on her face, she gestured for him to call her by placing her hand to her face as if she were talking on a phone. It was clear that her professional mode was an act. Cynthia was like a snake blending in with its territory. She fed off of Isaac's vibes and body language that her flirting was upsetting to Jasmine. As a result, put on her professional and uninterested act to keep the peace. She was a slick character.

Isaac walked Jasmine to his car and opened the passenger door for her. "He is such a gentleman," Jasmine thought to herself. As Isaac walked around to enter on the driver's side, he reached into his pants pocket and retrieved the copy of his receipt. To no surprise, Cynthia had written her contact number on it. Isaac placed the paper back in his pocket immediately because even though he knew Cynthia was playing a game, it caught him off guard. He didn't want to alert Jasmine because he knew he'd lose any points he'd gained with her thus far if she'd known that he'd accepted a contact number from the sexy waitress. Isaac didn't want Jasmine to get the wrong impression. He knew his charm smoothed the playing field, and he was not about to start from scratch. Isaac entered his vehicle and saw that Jasmine was smiling like a little girl ready to go get some ice cream for getting a good report card in elementary school. It was clear to Isaac that Jasmine was excited about going to his house. Isaac pulled away from the restaurant and revved his engine to show off its high horse power, and prepare to take off like a race car driver. As the rear tires screeched for about five seconds and the rear end fish tailed, everyone in the long line outside the restaurant turned their heads toward the thunderous noise that came from Isaac's stainless steel high performance muffler system. Most of the men were impressed with Isaac's stunt, but there were haters, too, who had nothing but negative comments to say about the expensive luxury sports car that Isaac was flossing in. "Look at that guy," they said. "He thinks he is all that! I bet you my car can beat his! That car is nice but it's not all that! It's going to take him 30 years to pay off that car! Look at that show-off!" Most of the women in line admired Isaac's car. They didn't know what kind of car it was, but they liked how it looked from the outside. They also appreciated the rumbling the powerful engine made as Isaac stepped on the gas pedal. They wished their boyfriends and husbands were successful enough to drive them around in that kind of car.

saac and Jasmine arrived at Isaac's home. Once again, he opened the passenger door so that Jasmine could exit his vehicle. Then he guided her through side entrance into the garage, and then into the home. "It smells so good in here," she said. "What's that wonderful aroma I smell?"

"It is my own concoction of scented oils," Isaac replied. "I use three scented oils, African-Musk, Good-Life, and China-Musk. I take all three and mix them with a dab of water; then I burn them until I'm ready to leave."

"We've been at that restaurant for a couple of hours now," said Jasmine, "and you still can smell that sweet and unique aroma."

Isaac could sense from Jasmine's body language that she was beginning to loosen up a bit and was attempting to get more comfortable around him, so he set the mood with some smooth jazz. He used a mixed CD. That way, if Jasmine didn't like a particular song, she was sure to like the next one. Isaac was trying to be as accommodating as possible because he wanted everything to be perfect for Jasmine. While the stereo played melodious tunes, Isaac pulled out his finest bottles of White Zinfandel and Chardonnay wines. Then he invited Jasmine to the spacious den on the first floor. Although it was summertime Isaac kept the central air conditioner in his house on high. It was obvious that Jasmine was a bit chilly as she folded her arms around her in an attempt to keep warm. Isaac wanted her to be as comfortable as possible. He lit the exotic fireplace and quickly brushed of the large Grizzly Bear rug. Isaac placed the wine bottles on the glass table and grabbed some frozen wine glasses from his freezer so that he didn't have to taint the wine with ice. Then he turned off the lights and allowed the flames from the fireplace to illuminate the room. "Oh my goodness," Jasmine thought. "He might be trying to entice me; I'd better watch him! This is too good to be true! I better watch how much wine I'm drinking. I wouldn't want this fine stud to slip me a Mickey." Jasmine was still excited, though, and having a good time with Isaac. She began to let her hair down and relax.

"Well, now that I've set the mood just right, I need to take my time," thought Isaac. "I'm going to take things slow." Isaac opened the corked wine bottles. As he poured the wine, he placed a white towel over his forearm with his palm down. Then he placed the bottle on top of the towel. Once he filled each glass, he ceased pouring by turning the bottle clockwise and in an upward motion, lifting the bottle upright not dripping any wine. Isaac poured wine like a professional at a wine-tasting event.

Jasmine marveled at how delicious Isaac made their drinks look. She noticed Isaac filled the glass close to its brim. As the two sat on the animal rug, sipped on fine wine and listening to smooth jazz, Jasmine became very relaxed. As Isaac struck up a conversation about the movies he enjoyed, he noticed Jasmine trying to ease off her shoes. "Let me help you with that!" he said as he slipped off Jasmine's shoes, revealing her manicured feet. "Wow Jasmine!" said Isaac. "You have beautiful feet!"

"Thank you," Jasmine responded as she smiled and took a grand swallow of wine. After about half an hour Isaac asked her if she'd like a friendly foot massage from being on her feet all day. "Sure," she said. "I don't get many foot massage invitations, so I'd better jump at this one!" Jasmine placed her bare feet on Isaac's lap. Isaac was already prepared as he leaned over toward the glass table and pulled a large bottle of scented massage lotion out from underneath it. Jasmine immediately noticed how organized Isaac was. She knew he was softening her up, but the wine had her on easy street. She was completely aware of what could come along with a sensuous foot massage. In the back of her mind, she was hoping Isaac was a rookie at giving foot massages. If the massage were mediocre, she would be able to resist any physical advances that might follow. Unfortunately for her, Isaac was skilled in the art of foot massage. He had strong but not overbearing hands. He never tickled the feet because he kept his fingernails cropped low, and he knew how to use his thumbs.

Isaac put a small amount of lotion in his palms and rubbed them in a circular motion, but not to the point of absorption. As he placed his hands on Jasmine's feet, he used his thumbs to move in a circular motion from her heel up to the top of her big toe. Isaac used the perfect amount of pressure, enough so that Jasmine could feel his thumbs through her aching foot arches without going to the bone. His hands were warm from the two of them being close to the fireplace, and then heat from the flames filled the room. The massage felt so good to Jasmine that her eyes rolled to the back of her head in pleasure. "Oh, Isaac that feels so good!" she moaned in approval. The more Isaac worked his slippery thumbs over her foot arch and his fingers between Jasmine's toes, the more she sighed in pleasure. Not many of Jasmine's past dates even rubbed her feet. The few who did couldn't light a match to Isaac at that point. "It's not just what you do; it's how you do it," she said to herself.

Isaac had Jasmine under a spell---the warm fireplace burning enough to make a baby fall asleep, the air filled with pleasant aromas, fine wines at their disposal, the best that smooth jazz has to offer, and a world-class foot massage. As time passed, Jasmine began to burn inside like the flames burning inside the fireplace. She developed a tingling sensation between her thighs (and she didn't have any sexually transmitted diseases). Before long, Jasmine's pleasurable moans from the foot massage turned into lustful moans. And of course, her alcohol consumption contributed to her feelings. As Jasmine gazed at Isaac, at that moment she wanted to become one with him in the way GOD intended only a married couple to become one. Those who become one this way prior to marriage GOD sees as committing a sin. Yes, I am talking about the three-letter word that many of us engage in prematurely---SEX! Jasmine's guard against Isaac was weakening. Isaac worked all the stress out of Jasmine's feet, and now she was ready for him to work out a few more areas that needed some attention.

Jasmine was well relaxed, grateful for the wonderful massage Isaac gave her. Isaac leaned back against the sofa as he sipped his glass of fine wine. At that moment, Jasmine leaned over slightly and planted a kiss on Isaac's cheek. Isaac turned to confront Jasmine. Next she planted a soft kiss on his lips. That was the green light for Isaac. He knew at that very moment Jasmine was more open and relaxed than she had ever been in his presence. Isaac leaned forward and returned Jasmine's kiss. Many women Isaac had previously been involved with considered him a good kisser. Isaac massaged Jasmine's lips with his in a slow seductive manner, and timed perfectly when to slip his tongue into her mouth to massage her tongue as well. Jasmine's mind was going wild. "This man can kiss like no other!" Jasmine thought. As the two kissed passionately, they moved close enough to each other to feel one another's natural curves. The two began to caress each other, raising their natural body temperature. By this time Jasmine was groping Isaac's well-defined muscles, and Isaac was hugging Jasmine's curvy body. The two began to undress one another as their lips stayed glued to each other. Not before long, the two were in their birthday suits.

There was no turning back now; they'd put themselves in a compromising position. The date started out innocent and friendly. Sure they were physically attracted to each other; that's how God made us. But it's up to us to make sound decisions on our own. And remember, situations like this take two to tango! Jasmine knew that being alone in the house with a man she was highly attracted to on their first date was not a good decision on her part. On the other side of the coin, Isaac knew that serving alcohol to Jasmine in his home while the two were alone also contributed to the lustful act of fornication. Either one of them could have prevented this sinful act by simply saying "no." Instead, the two made passionate love to each other for quite some time. They became one the way only husband and wife are meant to be one.

As they lay in each other's arms afterward, Jasmine was hoping that she had not acted too soon in sleeping with Isaac. She was presuming that Isaac would think of her as a promiscuous woman for going to bed with him on their first date. On the contrary, Isaac was cool, calm and collective. He lay there gazing at the fireplace as if what just happened between Jasmine and him was a normal episode. Jasmine had no idea what he was thinking, and it bothered her a little bit. She knew she'd lost control of herself. She knew there was a good chance that Isaac lost respect for her and would eventually play her like a wet food stamp. It was now 2:00 a.m., and Jasmine went to Isaac's bathroom to freshen up and get dressed to go home. When she returned to Isaac's living room, Isaac was dressed in black silk pajamas and a black robe to match. He walked over to her smoothly, kissed her on the lips, and asked if she was OK. She assured him that she was. Isaac walked her to the front door where her car was parked outside. Jasmine smiled, and they gave each other a long hug, for they both knew it was time for her to go home. "Call me when you get home and let me know you made it home safely," Isaac said. Jasmine nodded her head in approval, feeling better about how Isaac perceived her. After all, if he thought lowly of her, he wouldn't want her to call him at all. Jasmine walked outside, entered her car, and drove away.

Chapter 7

The

Aftermath

unday morning came, and Isaac decided to attend church to worship the Lord in spirit and in truth. Isaac got into the shower to wash thoroughly for the occasion. After he toweled off and shaved, he entered his master bedroom and put on one of his fine Italian cream and beige suits, with an ivory white dress shirt, and beige alligator shoes. Also, he wore the suit with a multi- colored tie of black, gold and white. To top the entire outfit, he placed a cream colored Derby style hat upon his head. Isaac walked to the full bodied mirror that was located in his upstairs hallway and gave a final look over and, he was so pleased with his image that he blew a kiss to himself and said aloud, "There it is!" He exited his home feeling good and well refreshed. Isaac entered his garage and pondered which vehicle he was going to take to church that day. He placed his right hand underneath his chin, caressing it as he contemplated. After several minutes he decided on the clean and shiny pearl white Cadillac, with beige leather seats, to match his suit. Not too flashy and not too dull. Just enough for a Sunday morning. Isaac pulled into the church parking lot filled with confidence. He exited his vehicle and walked toward the church entrance. All eyes were on him as he walked through the parking lot. He was the eye candy to the sisters of the congregation that morning, most of whom attended church every Sunday and were deeply rooted in God's word. But when they saw Isaac coming in they started singing "I Don't See Nothing Wrong With a Little Bump and Grind," By R. Kelly. Isaac knew he was looking good. As he entered the church, he greeted everyone with a smile and a firm handshake.

As Isaac took his seat in the back, the bell rung indicating that service was about to begin. A brother in the congregation approached the podium and asked the attendants to stand to be worded in prayer. Afterward, another brother led the singing with a voice so melodious that it would bring tears to one's eyes. Finally, the minister approached the podium to give the church the word. Isaac found himself squirming in his seat, uneasy because the minister was speaking on fornication that morning. The sermon was so powerful that it was as if he were talking directly to Isaac and no one else. The minister recited scriptures from the Holy Bible about how it is wrong for anyone to succumb to the temptations of the flesh. He went on about how marriage is honorable, and once man and woman are married the bed is undefiled. Everything the minister said made Isaac feel bad inside because he knew he was a fornicator. The words that came out of the minister's mouth forced Isaac to reflect on the many women he had sexual relations with, none of whom he was married to, and all the false promises he knew he wouldn't fulfill in rendering his hand in marriage. After all, Isaac knew deep down that many of them had sex with him hoping he would marry them. And even though he treated them with respect during the relationships, he didn't respect them enough to marry them. He just used that as leverage to get what he wanted. He was selfish and felt low inside because of it. Isaac could always remember something undesirable about the women he dated: they didn't make enough money, they weren't in shape, their hair wasn't long enough, they snored while they slept, they had children out of wed-lock, they wore too much make-up, or they didn't cook enough meals. Fact is, Isaac was entirely too picky when it came to women and he knew it now that he was more mentally mature. Isaac definitely had regrets and knew he was not completely fair with the women he'd dated. He was essentially a pimp with a conscience.

From that point on, Isaac promised himself he would always treat women with respect and be honest. That way they knew where he was coming from, and would not have any feelings of guilt if lust got the best of them. He made a pact with himself to never again mislead a woman to get what he wanted. But even though he had adopted this theory, he knew he was still wrong for engaging in premarital sex. But his newfound theory allowed him to feel better about how he operated as a person. He no longer saw himself as a villain because he put the ball in the woman's court when it came to intimacy. After the sermon, Isaac went home thinking subconsciously that he has to change his life around when it came to women and sex. Isaac was afraid that if he were to die at that very second, he might not make it through GOD's gates of Heaven. Many people who knew Isaac would have said he is as good as any good man, but Isaac was uncertain whether he would be good enough to make it into Heaven because of his past sexual relations.

Meanwhile, Jasmine was home talking on the phone with Monica. "So, how did your date go with Isaac?" Monica asked.

"Oh, it went really nice, girl," Jasmine answered. "Isaac is such a gentleman, and I really enjoyed myself!" Jasmine was trying to keep it short with Monica and change the subject because she felt uncomfortable about having sex with him on the first date. She thought she'd become more dignified and mature since college and was afraid Monica would see her as a tramp with no self-respect.

"That's all you have to say about your sexy date?" Monica responded in shock. "Why are you trying to change the subject on me, girl? Did Isaac hit it already or something?" There was a slight pause on the phone because Jasmine felt cheap that she had given up the panties to Isaac so quickly. Monica has been friends with Jasmine for at least 10 years now and knew when something was bothering her. Finally, Monica broke the silence. "Jasmine, you didn't go to bed with Isaac on the first date, did you?"

Jasmine reluctantly confirmed having intercourse. "Girl, I don't know what came over me that night," she said. Monica began cracking up. She laughed so loud that she was screaming screams that echoed throughout the house. In fact, Darius heard her all the way in the garage. He ran into the living room where Monica was still on the phone, fallen halfway off of the sofa, teary eyed from laughing so hard. Darius looked at the caller ID to see who was on the other line. Once he saw Jasmine's name, he moved his lips at Monica so Jasmine would not hear him. "What happened?" he mouthed.

"Your boy hit that on the first date!" Monica mouthed back. Darius put his hand over his mouth so, no one would hear him laugh, and he ran back down to the garage. Once he was there, he started shrieking and pounding his fist on the wall.

Monica got herself together where she would not be laughing in Jasmine's ear. "What happened that night, girl?" she asked. "Did he put it on you like that?"

Jasmine replied in a monotone voice, "Yeah, he put it on me, girl." Jasmine responded in a monotone voice. "It's strange, though, because at first I was mad because I caught him checking out our waitress as if he liked what he saw when he looked at her. So, my guard was up after that because he has wandering eyes and likes to look at other women. But he made up for it by ordering a wonderful main course for us. The food and the restaurant he selected were good, with the exception of our raunchy waitress. After we ate, girl, we went back to his house and let me tell you, girl, it was off the hook. He put on some smooth jazz, poured some wine, and dimmed the lights, and lit the fireplace. Isaac was really sweet, girl. Then to top things off, he gave me the best foot massage I've ever experienced. I was through, girl."

"Oh my goodness, girl," Monica responded. "Isaac rubbed those crusty dogs of yours that you call feet?"

Jasmine began to laugh and said, "My feet are fine; stop cracking on my feet!"

Monica was now fully interested in the details of Jasmine's date with Isaac. "What happened next, girl?" she asked. Jasmine started to loosen up a bit because she could hear the anxiety in Monica's voice.

Jasmine continued, "Isaac was irresistible after a few more glasses of wine and foot rubbing. I just had to kiss his full lips, so I did. Isaac kissed me back with authority, girl, and before I knew it, his tongue was in my mouth. He was kissing me so well that before I knew it all my clothes were off, all his clothes were off, and it was on like popcorn up in there. Isaac has a nice body, girl. He really knows how to please a woman. Before I knew it, it was two in the morning. I feel like a tramp!"

Monica assured Jasmine that she was not a tramp, but a lucky woman to have been courted by a most eligible bachelor such as Isaac. Unknowingly, Jasmine said just a little too much to Monica about her intimate encounter with Isaac, the man she always admired on the down low. Monica was always physically attracted to Isaac, but never let it be known out of respect for Darius. But after hearing from her best girlfriend how good a lover Isaac is, she wanted him more than she ever had. After talking some more with Jasmine about other things, Monica and Jasmine said goodbye and hung up the phone.

Meanwhile, Darius was inside the garage on his cell phone calling Isaac to ask how the date with Jasmine went. The phone rang four times before Isaac answered: "What's up, family?"

"Nothing much, man," Darius replied. "So, pimp, how did your date go with Jasmine?"

Isaac played it cool and low key as he answered, "Everything went pretty well, man. I mean the food was good and the atmosphere in the restaurant was smooth like Bailey's and cream on the rocks!"

"Man don't nobody want to hear all that corny stuff," said Darius.

"I want to know; did you get the goodies? And, no, I'm not talking about chocolate chip cookies."

Isaac started to laugh because he knew what "getting the goodies" meant.

"I knew my dog would come through like a champ," Darius said with excitement. "So how did the evening flow? I want to hear every little detail, man."

Isaac didn't feel comfortable about telling Darius about his and Jasmine's interlude. "Look, man, I really don't kiss and tell," he said.

Darius became frustrated with Isaac for not providing any explicit details about their sexual escapade. "Man, are you kidding me?" he said. "I introduced the two of you, man. Now you want to act like a scary punk that has never been with a woman before. Are you catching feelings for Jasmine or something? Did she put it on you that good that she has you hen pecked?"

"No it's not like that, man," replied Isaac. "I just don't want to talk about Jasmine like she is some trick off of the streets or something. I like her, and I really want to get to know her, man. So, be that as it may, you don't need to know any details about how her body looks naked or what some of her favorite positions are, man." That wasn't the response Darius was looking for, but he respected Isaac's stance to not kiss and tell, although he was very disappointed and even a little surprised at this shut-down approach Isaac had taken with him. He was used to being able to discuss almost anything with Isaac, but he realized that either Isaac was maturing or his interest in Jasmine was serious. He was happy for Isaac because he believed that Jasmine was a good candidate for marriage, but a little jealousy was in that mix, as well. Darius felt as though Jasmine had made Isaac respect their privacy because the other women in Isaac's life didn't mean enough to him, and in turn, he shared some details about their intimate moments. The two changed the subject and talked about sports for a while. Several moments later, they ended their conversation and hung up.

Darius ran upstairs and confided with his wife, Monica. "Hey Monica, what did Jasmine say about her date with Isaac?" he asked.

"Why haven't you asked Isaac yet?" asked Monica. Darius told her how Isaac failed to render any details about the date, and all he knew was that they had been intimate. Monica was surprised and even a little jealous because she thought Isaac had some positive feelings toward Jasmine even after her sleeping with him on the first date. Monica told her husband that Jasmine was also vague with her, and that all she knew for certain was that the two had "gotten busy" all night long. Monica began to wonder how she could experience what Jasmine experienced with Isaac. She still loved her husband, but they'd been married for several years, and Monica just wanted something new for a change---to be touched by someone who'd never touched her before, to be held and caressed by new arms and hands. She wanted to be picked up and made love to by someone entirely different from her husband. Monica wanted Isaac. In fact, she was so strongly driven by Jasmine's details of Isaac being a great lover that she became motivated to bring her thoughts and deep feelings to reality.

Monica lay in bed thinking of a master plan to get Isaac all to herself just for one night, day, evening, or lunch break. Hours had passed when in an instant, she propped herself up on the bed. "I got it," she said to herself. "This plan will work!"

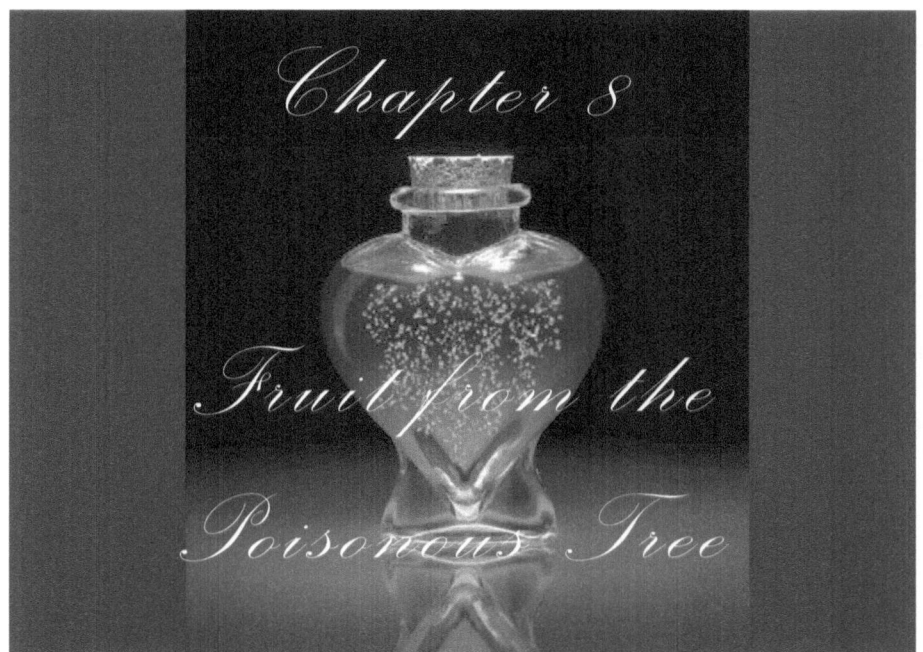

Chapter 8

Fruit from the
Poisonous Tree

A couple of weeks passed. Isaac and Jasmine had been dating each other quite consistently. Jasmine sincerely wanted to see her relationship with Isaac become more serious. Isaac liked Jasmine, but he was more comfortable just having sex with her on weekends. "Why should I buy the whole cow when I can get the milk for free?" he thought. In other words, because Jasmine was giving herself to Isaac on a regular basis, developing a meaningful relationship became less and less important to him.

One Friday evening, Isaac was doing his laundry. As he emptied his pockets of several pairs of pants he was preparing to wash, he pulled out an old receipt. Isaac unfolded the piece of paper and saw that it was Cynthia's phone number. He remembered all of her attractive physical attributes, how seductive she was when taking their order, and how she never blatantly disrespected his date in order to capture his attention. Isaac picked up his cell phone and rationalized, "There's no harm in calling her to see how she's been. I could thank her again for her fine service that night. After all, I'm not married or anything like that." Isaac dialed the number from the receipt. The phone rang four times before a woman answered. "Hello?"

Isaac was a little nervous as he replied, "Hello, may I please speak to Cynthia?"

"This is she," said the woman.

"You probably don't remember me," Isaac began, "But, this is Isaac. You were my waitress for me and my date one Friday evening a couple of weeks ago."

"You must be that fine handsome man that ordered the fancy and unique mixed drinks from the bar," Cynthia said with excitement. "Not to mention you were dressed in that tailor fitted navy blue suit."

Isaac began to blush on the other end. "Yes, that was me. I can't believe you have such a good memory."

"It was not hard for me to remember you," replied Cynthia, "because I don't give my phone number to just anybody. I am glad it's you. I started to think you weren't interested because I haven't heard from you since I served you at the restaurant."

"Oh, I've been busy over the last couple of weeks," Isaac explained. "I haven't had much time for anything but work."

Cynthia began to smile because she knew Isaac called her because he was interested. Smoothly and seductively, she baited Isaac. "Well since you have been so hard at work, why don't you and I hook up and relax? We could get something to eat, have a few drinks, and get to know each other better."

Isaac was really blushing now as he accepted the invitation. "Sure, I'd like that. I need a break. I look forward to seeing you again, Cynthia."

"So, your name is Isaac, and this is your cell phone number on my caller ID, right?" she asked.

"That's right!" Isaac replied.

"Well I know this lounge off the Boulevard that makes good food and serves nice mixed drinks," Cynthia suggested. "I know you appreciate mixed drinks, Sir Mix-a-Lot!" Now, she was just being silly.

"Sounds like a plan," confirmed Isaac. "So when would you like to do this?"

"Well I'm off tonight," Cynthia said, "so, if you don't have any plans, I could meet you there around 7."

"Do I have any plans tonight?" Isaac thought quickly. "OK, that's fine. Where is this lounge at again?" Cynthia gave Isaac detailed instructions on the location of the lounge. The two said goodbye, and the stage was set for them to meet later that evening. Isaac felt weary because Cynthia caught him off guard. He knew she had a strong character, and was appeased by her forthrightness. Isaac liked the fact that Cynthia knew what she wanted to do and just did it. Her spontaneous attitude was very alluring. Cynthia had a wild side and appeared fearless, and that strongly attracted Isaac.

It was no 6:00 p.m., and Isaac was showering up to meet Cynthia at the lounge. He began to ponder how the evening would go and what kind of approach he would use in setting the tone. At the same time, he was very confused because he thought by meeting up with Cynthia that he was being unfaithful to Jasmine. "I'm not in a committed relationship with anyone," he began to rationalize once again. "I'm just meeting Cynthia, not sleeping with her. So, what's the harm in having a couple of drinks?" Since Isaac could convince most women who didn't even know him to do just about anything, convincing himself to go on a date with an attractive free-spirited woman was all too easy. As he conned himself more and more, Isaac began to feel more comfortable with his decision to meet with Cynthia. Isaac was clean, polished, and dressed to impress. He jumped into his sports car and turned on some Tina Mary and Rick James tunes. "Give it To Me, Baby!" was blasting and the lyrics put Isaac in a particular mood to relax and to let the chips fall where they may. It didn't take long before he reached the lounge that Cynthia had chosen.

Isaac exited his vehicle and headed inside the lounge. The lounge had a sporty atmosphere inside. The interior lights were a bit loud and bright. The color scheme of the lounge was very colorful, as it included many of the teams of NBA, NFL, NHL and other major sports figures and logos plastered on its walls. The floor was of cherry oak wood tiles and the lounge had two spacious bars. One bar was modernized in dark brown and black leather throughout. The second bar was very flashy in bright orange, red, and white. Each bar had stainless steel stools with cushioned seats to match the color of their respective bar. Isaac heard "Early in the Morning" by the Gap Band playing in the background. Liking the selection, he started bobbing his head to the beat as he scanned the lounge for his date.

At first, he didn't see Cynthia. He walked gingerly to the more sophisticated bar, sat down at an available stool, and ordered a double shot of Grey Goose, pineapple juice, and cranberry juice on the rocks. The mix allowed him to relax as he waited for his hot date, as he listened to the juke box in the corner vibrate some of his most favorite songs from Marvin Gaye, Isaac Hayes, Smokey Robinson, and the Mary Jane Girls. About 30 minutes later, when Isaac was just a few sips away from finishing his drink, he looked at his watch to see how long he had been waiting. The moment he lifted his head from his time piece, there was a woman standing in front of him. Her identity didn't immediately register in Isaac's mind because his drink had already settled in his system. Everything in the lounge just seemed to slow down as he tried to confirm that the woman in front of him was his long-awaited date. As he focused his eyes on the figure in front of him, he saw a woman with a curvy body, wearing fitted jeans, a tight tailored top to match, and knee-high boots. Isaac looked the woman in the face, happy Cynthia had finally made it to the lounge. Isaac thought she looked even more appealing than she looked in her waitress uniform from the restaurant. Isaac took particular interest in the wavy ponytail that hung slightly below Cynthia's shoulders, with old-school bangs canted to the left side of her forehead.

"I'm so sorry I'm late, but traffic is jammed up," Cynthia apologized. Isaac began to smile as he stood to his feet, placed his hands gently upon hers, and guided her tenderly to the stool next to his. Cynthia began to smile.

"I thought for a minute you stood me up," Isaac replied, "but now that you're here, everything is OK." Cynthia began to blush and had a strong sense that Isaac really liked her. As she sat on the stool Isaac guided her to, Cynthia caught a whiff of the fragrance he was wearing.

"He smells so good," thought Cynthia. "Oh my goodness gracious!"

"What would you like to drink," Isaac asked Cynthia.

"I'd like one of your mixed drinks," she replied. Isaac began to laugh as he remembered placing his orders with her while she served him and Jasmine.

"OK no problem," Isaac replied. "I'll make you something that will relax you but not put you to sleep." Isaac signaled for the bartender to work her way over to their area so that he could place his unique order. Once the bartender made it to Isaac's stool Isaac whispered in her ear what he wanted Cynthia to sip on. The bartender raised her eyes in amazement as she took the special order. Once the waitress returned, she placed the requested drink in front of Cynthia. It was an ocean blue drink with ice in it and a slice of orange on the rim of the glass, holding a skinny straw. "What's this drink called?" Cynthia said in excitement. "It looks so pretty!"

"Don't worry about that," replied Isaac. "Just enjoy it, and most importantly, sip on it. You don't want to gulp a powerful drink like this one in a hurry. It may ruin your night with a DWI case!"

Cynthia brought the straw up to her lips to taste this concoction of Isaac's, sipping ever so gently on the straw. As the straw changed colors as the drink flowed from the glass and filled her mouth, Cynthia's eyes lit up with delight as the sweet ingredients danced on her taste buds. "This is very good," said Cynthia. "What's in it again?"

Isaac began to laugh as he replied, "I told you not to worry about what's in the drink. It's a secret, and it's strong, so please sip on it." Isaac sensed that Cynthia had a strong-willed personality since she tried to get the ingredients twice in a subtle manner.

Cynthia continued sipping on the blue concoction. Isaac struck up a conversation as the music played. "I run a non-profit organization that helps extend resources throughout the community," Isaac began. "One day I want to become a full-blown politician working on Capitol Hill in Washington, D.C." he exclaimed.

Cynthia was impressed by Isaac's vision. "It's good to see a young African American setting admirable goals for himself," she said. "Not many brothas have a positive outlook on life and just flat out lack focus on their careers," she added.

"Yeah, I always wanted to make America a better place to live," Isaac replied. "I figure what more effective way to change the world than to be a politician with the authority to help establish policy for all to follow?"

Cynthia began to tell Isaac about herself. "Well, besides waitressing at night, I go to college full time and raise my six-year-old daughter, Myra," she began. "My mother is a big help in helping raise my daughter since I had her at such a young age. This allows me to attend college full time at New York University," Cynthia continued. "Right now I'm pre-law, but I don't really know what I want to do yet. I'm thinking of becoming a Lawyer or even going into forensics, the technological side of law enforcement."

Isaac though Cynthia was interesting and had respectable goals in life, as well. "Wow, I had no idea you even attended college," Isaac said.

"What's that supposed to mean?" Cynthia asked.

"No offense or anything like that," Isaac explained, "but you just don't look like the type to attend NYU. I mean NYU is an Ivy League college, and people who attend there have exceptional SAT scores.

I'm not saying you don't look intelligent enough to get accepted into such a prestigious college, but you look more Spellman University bound, very sexy first, and smart like that on the down-low second."

Cynthia smiled even though she thought it was a poor excuse for a compliment. Isaac knew what he said to her was stereotypical and even degrading. But being a great mood changer, he rose to his feet and asked Cynthia to follow him to the dance floor. Cynthia took one long sip of her drink and grabbed Isaac's hand as he guided her to the lounge's dance floor. He placed his hands gently upon her waist, and Cynthia draped her arms over his shoulders. The two began to dance so well together, one would have thought they'd been dancing with each other for years, their bodies moving in unison to "Flowers." The more they danced, the better they moved together. Their bodies intertwined like two snakes winding in the sand as they made love to one another. Some bystanders looked at them in awe and some in envy. Cynthia and Isaac were in their own world as they rocked their bodies to the funky beat. Cynthia closed her eyes as Isaac pulled her in even closer. He could smell the wonderful scent of perfume on her neck as she caressed his firm, well-developed shoulders. Isaac was thinking "What a thorough woman she is," while Cynthia was thinking, "I could do some things with this man."

After a few songs, Isaac led Cynthia back to their seats. Unfortunately, the lounge was crowded by this point, and their seats were no longer available. Isaac leaned over slightly and whispered in Cynthia's ear, "It's getting tight in here. Can you think of a place where we can go to get better acquainted?"

Cynthia smiled and said, "Sure, I don't live too far from here, and we could even stop for Chinese take-out if you'd like."

Isaac started getting excited, but he held it inside as he responded in a calm fashion. "Sounds like a plan. I'll meet you out front and I'll follow you."

As the two worked their way through the crowd, Cynthia was leading the way while Isaac trailed behind her holding her hand. Her hips swayed from side to side as she walked, just like a model on the cat walk. As each of her heels touched the ground, her leg and calf muscles flexed. And she smelled so good when they danced. At that point, Isaac wondered how it would be to become one with Cynthia. When they finally made it outside the lounge, Cynthia pointed to her car and told Isaac to meet her there. Isaac walked to his car, which was parked down the street. As he drove up to Cynthia's car, he flashed his headlights to let her know that he was ready to go. Cynthia waved her hand out the window to acknowledge his signal. Cynthia drove as Isaac followed. They stopped at a Chinese take-out spot to order food, but food was not on either of their minds.

Chapter 9

Out of Bounds

efore long, Isaac and Cynthia had their Chinese take-out and arrived at Cynthia's condo. Isaac was still tipsy from the liquor he consumed at the lounge while Cynthia was open like a Wal-Mart store on Black Friday. As the two entered Cynthia's two-bedroom loft, they walked upstairs to a very spacious, open-plan-style condo. "I like your spot, Cynthia!" Isaac said.

"Thank you so much, Isaac," Cynthia replied. "Why don't you let me show you around?" Cynthia led Isaac to the spacious kitchen, which revealed a large round mahogany table with six chairs to match. The surface was very shiny, and in the middle of the table was a wooden vase with exotic flowers in it. The countertops were made of a black, shiny laminated material, and the stainless steel stove was large and shined radiantly. An oval rug lay in front of the oven and the sink displayed a silver shiny gooseneck faucet. And Cynthia kept it all so clean!

As Cynthia showed Isaac each room in the loft, her shoes clanged on the beautiful hardwood floors, like a horse prancing on the streets during a parade, her leg muscles vibrating slightly with each step. This drove Isaac absolutely crazy. Isaac continued to compliment Cynthia on her beautiful place and choice of decor. And she enjoyed showing her place to a man who appreciated her taste.

As they entered the living room, Cynthia turned on her 60" flat-screen Sony TV, complete with surround sound, to a smooth R&B channel, and the two listened to Musiq Soul Child. As they moved into the master bedroom, Isaac appreciated Cynthia's thick, yet firm mattresses, and tiger-printed sheets. Shades of brown and beige accented the entire room. Isaac sat on the edge of the bed. "This bed feels pretty comfortable," he observed. "I bet you sleep well at night, don't you?"

Cynthia paused for a minute, thinking about his question, and then responded in a serious tone, "It doesn't matter how cozy the bed is when you're the only one in it and you long for someone to share it with." Isaac read the message in Cynthia's response loud and clear. As beautiful and as sexy as she was, she longed for a mate to share herself with. Isaac pounced on that moment like an eagle on a mouse. He extended his arm and hand in a gesture for her to sit with him on the bed. Cynthia turned her head slightly to the left but kept eye contact with Isaac. She slightly smiled and walked over to Isaac to hold his extended hand.

As Cynthia grabbed Isaac's hand, he pulled her next to him on the bed. "I think you're beautiful and you don't have to be alone if you don't want to," he said urgently. "I'm here for you, baby, right now!" As Cynthia looked Isaac in the eyes, he put his arms around her waist and caressed her snug. Cynthia slightly sighed; his touch was perfect. Isaac felt her melt in his arms and moved in for the kill. He leaned forward and kissed her softly on the neck. Then he planted another kiss on her jaw bone, which was followed by another on her cheek. Finally, he kissed her square on her juicy lips. Cynthia sighed in pleasure and kissed him back. Isaac knew beyond a shadow of a doubt that he had her. He remained very smooth, though, as he kept his composure and took his time. He began kissing her more passionately, and Cynthia's head moving from side to side in a slow, passionate motion. Isaac guided their bodies to lie on the spacious bed they were already sitting on. Cynthia's loins were starting to heat up because his body felt so good against hers. Cynthia rolled her body on top of Isaac's rather aggressively. "Oh-Oh," Isaac thought. "What have I gotten myself into here?" Then he remembered what his father told him when he was 18: "Son, think long and hard about what you pursue in life. You may get it." As each second passed by, Cynthia became more anxious and rough. She couldn't get Isaac's shirt off fast enough, ripping three buttons off in the process. "Wait a minute, baby," Isaac said. "Let me do it; you're ruining my shirt."

"I'm sorry," Cynthia said under her breath as she continued groping and caressed Isaac. This made Isaac a little uncomfortable because he knew he was no longer in control of the steamy situation. He was beginning to feel physically helpless, and even violated. Isaac was slowly but surely feeling like a victim of circumstances. He was in another woman's home, in her bedroom, doing what she wanted him to do. Isaac was like a fish out of water because he was so used to controlling his encounters on his own turf.

Cynthia, on the other hand, was a thoroughly built woman who exercised four to five days a week and did not know her own strength. As she straddled Isaac, she began taking off his belt. Isaac felt her great strength as she tugged at it. He knew she'd ruin his leather belt if he didn't say something, so he placed his hands on hers and said, "Here, let me get that for you. Take it easy, Cynthia. It's not that serious, baby!" Cynthia allowed him to remove his own belt, but she didn't give up her dominant full-mount position. She was like a spider in its web on top of its prey. Isaac didn't want to seem like a punk, so he put his arms around her waist again and kissed her on her neck to try to regain control. But Cynthia was too hot at that point and Isaac wasn't moving fast enough for her. She sucked on Isaac's neck so violently that he looked like he'd been attacked by jellyfish. Cynthia hopped off Isaac for a brief moment and yanked his pants off from the bottom, and they came off Isaac's legs like a disappearing act at the circus. By this time, Isaac began to feel like a rape victim. "Calm down a little," he said once again.

"OK, I'll be gentle," she said with a determined look on her face. She quickly undressed herself and remounted Isaac. The two became one, with Cynthia leading the way and Isaac in tow. Cynthia was only interested in fulfilling her needs her way, even if it meant using and abusing Isaac. By the time their sexual escapade was over, Isaac was left confused about what exactly happened to him. Even though he wanted to sleep with Cynthia, he didn't appreciate being treated like a piece of meat, a tool, or an inexperienced lover. Cynthia, on the other hand, felt wonderful and had no regrets. After all, she'd just received a full dose of someone she was highly attracted to. She maneuvered him into her environment where she could be in total control and have her own way.

Isaac entered Cynthia's bathroom and turned on the shower. As the steam filled the room, Isaac looked at himself in the mirror, wondering what just happened. He started laughing for fear that he might cry if he didn't. As Isaac entered the steamy shower, the water was so hot it nearly scorched him. Isaac hollered like a ware wolf and immediately turned the hot water down. Cynthia entered the bathroom, concerned about what made Isaac scream in such a high pitched tone. "Is every-thing OK in here, sweetie?" she asked.

Still trying to be masculine about the situation, Isaac said in a deep voice, "Sure, I'm fine; the water was just a little hot!"

"OK, I'll get our plates together," Cynthia replied, "so when you're done freshening up you can come eat some Chinese food!"

Cynthia exited the bathroom to give Isaac some privacy. Isaac took a wash cloth and the bar of soap lying on the soap dish and began to scrub his body vigorously as if he'd been infected with a skin disease. He felt dirty and wanted to make sure he got Cynthia's essence off of him. About 20 minutes later, Isaac exited the shower and began to towel dry off, thinking of ways to get out of there as fast as he could. He was simply embarrassed about being dominated by Cynthia. As Isaac started to get dressed, Cynthia entered the bathroom with a devilish grin on her face. Isaac knew Cynthia wanted him again "Oh my God," he thought. "Does this woman ever get enough?" Cynthia grabbed Isaac's underwear to prevent him from putting them on and pushed him up against the sink. She began kissing him on his neck and face. Isaac told her he was tired and hungry and wanted her to stop. But Cynthia ignored him. "Just give me 10 more minutes, Isaac!" She was physically strong and mentally determined to have her way with him one more time. Isaac could have overpowered her if he'd wanted to, but he knew if he physically resisted Cynthia someone would get hurt. So, Isaac allowed her to have her way with him right there in her spacious bathroom. This wasn't the most pleasant intimate experience Isaac ever had. Cynthia brought herself to another climax using her new man-toy. Once again, Isaac entered the shower and scrubbed his body vigorously. After he exited, he put his clothes on as fast as he could. One minute hadn't passed by the time he was fully dressed.

Isaac entered the living room where Cynthia was dressed in a gold colored robe. Individual tables were set up for their Chinese cuisine. "I heated the food up, and your dish should be hot and ready to eat," she said, grinning from ear to ear, gleaming with joy. She looked like she'd just won the lottery.

"Thank you," Isaac said, as he sat down to eat.

Cynthia could tell by the expression on Isaac's face that he was uncomfortable. "Are you OK, honey?" she asked.

"Yeah, I am just really tired and my stomach is bothering me," he responded.

Cynthia played along as if she understood Isaac. She knew deep down that he didn't like what just happened. "Can I turn the TV channel?" he asked as they consumed their dinner. Cynthia handed him the remote, and Isaac immediately turned to ESPN's Sports Center, hoping it would take his mind off their sexual escapade. As he ate his food and watched the program, he said little to Cynthia as she studied his body language. It was clear to her that Isaac couldn't wait to leave her home. Cynthia waited for Isaac to finish his plate and then gathered up the empty Chinese food cartons and discarded them. Meanwhile, Isaac was trying to figure out how much time he was going to let pass before he said good night to Cynthia. He didn't want to appear ungrateful by leaving too quickly; after all, she'd just fed him dinner.

Cynthia sat down next to him. "I can tell something is bothering you, Isaac. What is it?" she asked. "You can be honest with me." Isaac was caught off guard by Cynthia's questioning. Cynthia could see the confusion on his face and decided to make it easy on him. "Did I come on to you too strong?" she asked.

Isaac broke down and told her what was on his mind. "Yeah, Cynthia, you are way too aggressive, man." He confessed. "You practically raped me in here!"

Cynthia looked down in disappointment. It was clear to her that Isaac didn't want to be involved with her after that night. Then she looked back into Isaac's eyes and said, "I didn't mean to disrespect you in any way. I thought that from your body language and the way we were connecting, that you wanted me the way I wanted you."

"I was feeling you very much, and I was thinking about becoming intimate with you, but not exactly the way it happened," Isaac replied.

Cynthia knew Isaac found her too overbearing, so she apologized once again. "Look, Isaac, I really like you, and I thought we were on the same page, but apparently there was a huge miscommunication between us," she said. "I guess this is why the rule of thumb is never to sleep with someone on the first date. I made the mistake and I'll live with it. I'm sorry if I gave you the wrong impression, and I understand if you don't want anything more to do with me. But I hope you can find it in your heart to forgive me and start over. I know you want to leave now, so I won't hold you back. Just think about what I said, and if I don't hear from you, I will understand the decision you've made."

Isaac gathered his jacket, gave Cynthia a hug, and exited her home, knowing he didn't want anything more to do with her. He found himself wondering who else she'd victimized. How many other people has she slept with on the first date? Isaac was completely sold on the idea that Cynthia was an absolute freak and would sleep with whoever she could get her legs around. Strangely enough, Cynthia felt deep down that she was entirely too aggressive and anxious in her approach to being intimate with Isaac and knew he didn't want anything to do with her after that evening.

Chapter 10

Rebound

t was Sunday afternoon, and Isaac had just returned home from church. It had been a long week for him, and he barely remembered what the sermon was about, even though he felt spiritually rejuvenated each time he attended church. As Isaac neatly draped his Sunday suit over a hanger and hung it in his closet, his cell phone rang. He walked into the kitchen, picked it up off the counter top and saw that it was Jasmine on the caller ID. His heart raced with excitement. He was glad it was Jasmine and not Cynthia. "Hello, Jasmine," Isaac answered. "How are you doing? It's been a while since I heard from you, and it's so good to hear from you!"

"Yeah right," Jasmine responded. "You haven't called me in over a week now," she said jokingly. "You must be really busy these days," she said. "I know how things can get between your career and other responsibilities after hours."

"Yeah, things have been a bit busy around here for me," Isaac said, "But I always have time for Jasmine. Would you like to meet for dinner or go to a movie tonight?" he asked.

"Well my girlfriend is having something at her house this evening," she replied. "I think you're friends with her husband, Darius."

Isaac paused for a moment. "Oh, that's right," he responded. "They're having a get –together to honor their four-year anniversary. I've been so busy that I almost forgot about that."

"Well, I could meet you there if you like," Jasmine said.

"I'd much rather pick you up at your place and we could go together if that is all right with you," Isaac said.

Jasmine grinned from ear to ear. "OK," she said excitedly. "Pick me up around six." Jasmine gave him her address and hung up.

After Isaac hung up with Jasmine, he called Darius. The phone rang three times. "Hello?" Darius answered.

"What's good, my people?" said Isaac. "How have you been, man? Are you guys ready for tonight?"

"Oh, you do remember my number," Darius answered back annoyed. "I thought you lost it since I haven't heard from you in a few weeks. You didn't even call to let me know how your date with ol' girl went. What was her name again? You know who I'm talking about…the waitress lady."

Isaac remembered he'd told Darius that he was going out with Cynthia and that he didn't call with any details. Isaac wanted to forget all about that miserable night. "Aw, man, it wasn't that serious," he said trying to downplay the whole evening. "Besides, I've been so busy that I really haven't had much time for anything. I haven't even been in touch with Jasmine."

"Bump that," Darius said, returning to the subject of the date with Cynthia. "I want to know what went down with you and the Cynthia, joint. This is not like you, man. You always call and let me know what went down after any date, so either the date went really good or really bad. Which is it?"

Isaac paused for a few seconds as Darius listened. Then Isaac broke down and told him what happened. "Man, that woman is a beast," he said. "I think she abused me."

Darius dropped the phone. Isaac could hear him laughing extremely loud in the background for several minutes. He was trying real hard to see the humor, but no matter how hard he tried to even get a smile out of the situation, he couldn't. After all, he was embarrassed about Cynthia taking advantage of him that night. Darius got himself together and forced himself to stop laughing. Then he picked up the phone and said, "That's a good thing, right?" he asked. "That woman got down to the nitty-gritty with you, man. Isn't that what you wanted?"

"Yeah, but not like that, man," Isaac responded. "She made me feel like a piece of meat. She was strong and I really didn't have a choice, man. I even told her 'no,' and she kept going."

Darius dropped the phone again, and Isaac could hear him cracking up in the background. Now, Darius was stomping his feet on the ground trying to control his laughter. Isaac was on the other end becoming frustrated, sorry that he told Darius anything about that awful night. Isaac didn't want to seem like a little girl to his boy, Darius, so he changed up his attitude so Darius wouldn't suspect that Cynthia punked him.

When Darius finally picked the phone back up from laughing so hard, he said, "Are you serious, man? You're crazy. So, really, you are the man once again. Just another notch on your belt. Tagged another one."

Isaac went along with Darius to save face. "True, true," he responded. "I am the man once again. Sometimes I have to actually beat these women off me, man."

Darius lost any suspicion after Isaac's statement because for years Isaac has been getting women in and out of bed like a legendary Mack. He would never suspect that Isaac could ever be taken advantage of by another woman. "So, what time are you planning to come over tonight, man?" asked Darius. "Monica and I have a real nice spread for the guests tonight. I can't believe I've been married for four years now. It seems like yesterday when I proposed to her. Where did the time go?"

"Congratulations on your anniversary, man," Isaac said. "You deserve a good woman like Monica. I hope you guys continue to grow and be prosperous. I'm picking up Jasmine around 6, and we'll be at your house shortly after that."

"Sounds good, man," Darius said. "I'll see you guys around 6:30 then." The two hung up, and Isaac looked at the clock and saw that it was only 2. So, he decided to take a nap for a few hours. He was mentally drained; he was just beginning to feel the physically draining effects of being a victim of date rape. No matter how hard he fought to get the incident out of his mind, Isaac was still traumatized by what Cynthia had done.

Isaac slept for a couple of hours before he was awakened by a knock at the door. He got out of his bed and walked to the window to see who was there. He was happy to see that it was Jasmine. He put on some jeans and a white t-shirt. As he opened the door, Jasmine was standing there with a smile on her face. "I know you were expected to meet me at my house later on, but I had to see you sooner," said Jasmine.

Isaac didn't mind seeing Jasmine's beautiful face so early. "No problem at all, Jasmine. Would you like to come inside and sit down while I get ready for the anniversary party?" Isaac responded. Jasmine entered the house, took her jacket off, and placed it on the sofa in the living room. "Would you like something to drink while you wait?" asked Isaac.

"Sure," replied Jasmine. "I'd love something to drink just as long as it's not too strong. You had me trippin' the last time I was here."

Jasmine started to laugh as she recollected what happened on their first date. "I completely understand what you mean," Isaac said. "You don't want to show up at Darius and Monica's party intoxicated before everything gets started. I'll pour you a glass of wine, something a little sweet and not too strong, just the way I like my woman!"

Jasmine smiled and looked down as if something was on her mind. Taking note of the gesture, Isaac turned on "Fortunate" by Maxwell. Afterward, he pulled out a wine glass and popped open a bottle of Pinot

Grigio. Isaac liked setting the mood, and he wanted Jasmine to feel relaxed around him. He knew there was something she was afraid to tell him. Isaac reached into his refrigerator and grabbed a bag of strawberries. He walked over to the kitchen countertop, rinsed the strawberries off in the sink, and placed them in a bowl. Then he placed the glass of wine on the table next to the sofa in the living room and asked if she could sit in the chair where he placed the glass. Jasmine got up from the sofa and sat down at the table. Isaac began to pour the wine and placed the bowl of strawberries on the table next to her. "Here's a little fruit to go with such splendid wine, sweetheart," he said.

Jasmine gasped for air. "Oh, you are so sweet," she said. "You didn't have to go through all this trouble!"

"Really, it's no problem at all," Isaac responded. "You go ahead and enjoy the strawberries." Isaac walked upstairs to get dressed for the much-anticipated party. As he left the living room, the stereo began to play "Come Home to Me" by Anthony Hamilton.

Isaac's music was quite moving and inspirational to Jasmine. And the wine she was sipping and the strawberries she was munching just added to the mental rollercoaster she was on. Isaac's goal to get Jasmine to relax while she waited for him to get dressed was accomplished, however. After 20 minutes of waiting, Jasmine was feeling pretty nice. She wasn't intoxicated, but she was feeling warm inside and more eager to say what was on her mind. Isaac walked down his stairs and could tell by Jasmine's body language that she was feeling better, bobbing her head to the rhythm of the songs being played. "Awww yeah, this is my jam!" she yelled while raising her hands in the air. Isaac knew that now was a good time to find out what was on her mind. Isaac danced his way over to where Jasmine was sitting and poured himself a glass of wine. As he joined her at the table, he began to sip on his wine, and the two began bobbing their heads to the music together. Jasmine took a good look at what Isaac was wearing and complimented him on his outfit. She paid special attention to Isaac's navy blue alligator shoes with his matching designer blue Sean John dress jeans, beautifully paired with a white buttoned dress shirt with window-pane designs. Isaac thanked Jasmine for the compliment and then returned the attention. He noticed how the burgundy and gold cat-suit hugged the curves of her body, how her bare back was displayed, and how the lace shoulder straps revealed some of her soft skin. "You look very nice tonight, too, Jasmine," Isaac said. "I love your choice of clothes."

"Thank you," Jasmine replied.

Isaac moved a little closer to Jasmine and placed his hand on her knee. "I can tell something is on your mind," he said. "Just keep it real and let me know what you're thinking about."

Jasmine nodded and said, "Yeah, you're right. Something has been on my mind lately. Ever since you and I met, I have been attracted to you, and I know you're attracted to me. Then we go on this date and I know I had a good time with you, but then we moved way too fast and slept together. Originally I was fine with the decision I made in having sex with you, but I haven't heard from you in so long. If I hadn't called you today, I wouldn't have known whether you even wanted to be in the same room with me ever again. The truth of the matter is, I don't know where I stand with you, Isaac. I don't know what you want from me, if anything at all. Can you see us being in a relationship one day, or was our first date all that will ever be? I just want to know how feel about me."

Tears formed in her eyes as she spoke to Isaac. Jasmine was putting her heart on the line by telling Isaac how she felt about the two of them, and asking where they were going in the future. Isaac appreciated this side of Jasmine. She was sincere and most of all, honest, humbled by the entire situation of not knowing for sure if she'd ruined any chance of having a serious relationship with Isaac by going to bed with him on the first date.

Isaac felt in his heart that Jasmine would be a good match for him. He liked her style and her emotions. Jasmine was not puffed up with boasting or bragging about herself. And the only thing Jasmine was self-ish about was wanting Isaac all to herself in a meaningful relationship.

She wasn't looking at him as a sex object; her feelings were more genuine than that. Isaac placed his arm halfway around Jasmine's shoulder and began to stroke her lightly across her back. "Look, I'm sorry for not reaching out to you these last few weeks," he said. "But I've been going through so many things lately. I heard what you said, and I feel what you said. And if it's all right with you, I'd like to be in a relationship with you and see where we go. If we want to figure out whether we are meant to be together, first we have to acknowledge that we're in a relationship with each other. So, if it is OK with you, you are my lady and I am your man!" As a natural leader, Isaac liked being in charge, but not in a dictatorial manner.

Jasmine looked in Isaac's eyes and started to laugh. "Oh, now you're my boyfriend?" she said sarcastically. "We go together? You're my main squeeze? We're going steady now?" she continued, being silly. Isaac began to laugh, too. "You are so cute," Jasmine said. "You're my man now." Even though Jasmine thought Isaac's approach to making their relationship official was a bit elementary, it was what she had been yearning for since the two had been together. They kissed each other and then finished drinking their wine and eating the strawberries. Afterward, Isaac said, "Would you like for me to drive, or do you want to do the honors of escorting us to the party?"

"You can drive baby!" replied Jasmine.

Isaac led her to the garage and said, "Let's take the Aston Martin this evening! It matches your outfit!" Isaac opened the passenger door so she could enter. Isaac walked around to the driver's side after making sure Jasmine's seat belt was buckled and her door was shut securely. Isaac mashed a button next to his rearview mirror, which opened the garage door so he could exit. Isaac then turned on the sounds of Aaron Hall on the car stereo. As he slowly backed out of the garage, Jasmine looked at Isaac and smiled slightly in approval in his choice of music. As they cleared the garage, Isaac mashed another button near his rearview mirror to close the garage door behind them, and the two were on their way to the anniversary party at Darius and Monica's house.

Chapter 11

Aphrodisiacs

at Their Best

wenty-five minutes later, Jasmine and Isaac pulled up in front of Darius and Monica's house. Monica was watching Isaac through her upstairs bedroom window as she continued to get ready for the party. Isaac exited his car and walked smoothly to the passenger side. He opened the door for Jasmine to exit, and when Monica realized it was her best friend getting out of the car, she became envious and even a little jealous. Monica walked across her bedroom to the bathroom to make sure her make-up was flawless and adjusted her outfit to ensure that her bodily assets were noticeable. First, she adjusted her bra to hoist her breasts up and made sure that her G-String wasn't showing through her fitted suede dress pants. Next, she made sure that her toenail polish wasn't chipped as she slid on her sexy high heels to match her outfit. She then fluffed her hair to make sure it was properly balanced. At this point, any man with half a brain would find her irresistible. Just as Monica turned off the light in the bathroom, Darius entered to let her know most of the guests arrived. When Monica walked out of the bathroom and Darius saw how seductive she was dressed, he said, "Well, well, well, look at you. Who are we trying to impress this evening? You never dress this sexy for me!"

"Oh will you stop nagging at me," replied Monica. "First you complain that I don't dress sexy enough for you, and then when I do dress nice for you, you complain that I'm dressed too provocatively. I am damned if I do and damned if I don't with you. That's why we argue all the time."

"Maybe you are right," said Darius. "I need to stop being so insecure, baby. It's just that ever since you caught me cheating on you two years ago with my tramp psychologist, I really haven't been able to think straight. I'm very insecure when it comes to you, Monica. I know that you've forgiven me for the affair, but part of me feels that if you were given the perfect opportunity to cheat on me with the right person, you would jump on it in a heartbeat."

"Now see, you've done so much dirt during this marriage," responded Monica, "that you can't even allow yourself to be happy and comfortable in your own home on our anniversary. Now you got me thinking about all the times you told me you were working late at the job or going out with the fellas. Meanwhile, you were getting your money's worth in psychology fees. I can't believe you had sex with that crossed-eyed wench. It was bad enough we had to fork out thousands of dollars for you to seek help because you couldn't keep your manhood in your pants. I handpicked the psychologist myself. I made sure she was hard on the eyes. I mean she was buck-toothed, bald-headed, and crossed-eyed. I knew there was no way you would be attracted to her. But you still managed to sleep with her while you were supposed to be getting help for your sex addiction. I'm trying real hard now to have a good time and put our differences aside for one evening. I'm dressed for you because you always tell me you like it when I look like a street walker. Well, here I am, Darius, dressed to impress you. Now if this is too sexy for you, let me know now and I'll spend another hour choosing something else to wear!"

Darius could tell Monica was disturbed about his insecurity, but he didn't want the guests to wait any longer. Obviously he'd lost the right to try to tell Monica what to wear since he'd been caught in several affairs during their four-year marriage. And he knew he had an attractive wife who could even the score at the snap of her fingers. After all, many men would love to be married to Monica or even be with her for just one evening.

"Well, then, all right, honey," Darius finally said about Monica's designer Chanel outfit, "I support you and all that you do. You look very nice this evening!"

"Thank you, honey," replied Monica. "Now, let's get downstairs and greet our guests. Oh, and honey, get your drink all the way on; you need to relax."

"Wow, I have the best wife in the world!" Darius exclaimed. "I got my freak on with other women and she never divorced me, and now she's begging me to get drunk at our anniversary party. I got it made. Now, let me get down there and see some of these fine women!" Darius thought. "You know, honey," he finally said to Monica, "you are so understanding. I do need to relax and believe me I intend to get my drink on. I'll see you down stairs, baby," said Darius as he left the room.

After Darius went downstairs, she listened to her crowd of guests from upstairs as they congratulated Darius on his anniversary. Then Monica went down to make her grand entrance. All the men were checking her out, amazed at how beautiful she looked that night. Most men were thinking how lucky Darius was to be married to Monica, especially the ones who got wind of him having affairs with other women. As Monica walked across the room, most of the ladies there knew she looked good and had it going on. They also knew their men were scoping her out. As Monica greeted her guests, each congratulated her on her anniversary. Then she crossed Jasmine's path and the two of them started screaming like two wild alley cats in excitement. "Oh, my God, girl, you look astonishing tonight!" Jasmine screamed. "You've been working out and everything!"

"Thank you, girl. You look good, too," replied Monica. "I see you been doing the damn thing too!"

Jasmine smiled and thanked her for the compliment. "Happy anniversary, girl!" she said. "How long have you been married now?"

"Four years now," Monica replied. "It went by so fast, girl. It seems like yesterday I was walking down that aisle with my dad shaking like a leaf as he walked with me to give me away to Darius."

Jasmine was genuinely happy for her Monica because she truly believed she was happily married. Jasmine gave her a final hug and congratulated her once again. "Let me get some of this grub while you make your rounds here," said Jasmine.

"OK, girl," replied Monica. "Oh, by the way, who did you come with?

"My new man, Isaac," responded Jasmine, beaming with joy as those words came out of her mouth.

"Your new man?" inquired Monica. "What? Y'all go together now?"

"Yeah, that's my Boo Boo now!" exclaimed Jasmine in excitement.

Monica was even more jealous now, but she played it all the way off with a smile and said, "That's just too cute. I'm so happy for you guys!"

Jasmine thanked her and walked over to Isaac, who was standing by the food table getting a snack. Monica followed Jasmine so she could get a better look at Isaac and to formally greet him.

Monica swung her hips as she walked toward Isaac, smiling so hard that one could count all of her white teeth. When Isaac saw how seductive Monica looked in her outfit, he stopped chewing the food he was eating. Monica picked up on Isaac's expression and knew he liked what he saw. Jasmine totally missed the nonverbal interaction between the two. Monica very confidently held out her hand for Isaac and waited for him to congratulate her. Isaac fell for the bait, grabbed Monica's hand, and said, "Congratulations on your anniversary, Monica. You look so good, girl. Look at you."

Monica was feeling real good about herself as she thanked Isaac for the compliment. As Isaac tried to release her hand, Monica held on to his snuggly but not too tight. After all, she didn't want to alarm Jasmine of her inappropriate action. Then she smiled and said, "So I hear that you and my girl, Jasmine, are officially in a relationship now."

"Yes. Man, word gets around pretty fast around here," replied a smiling Isaac.

Jasmine was still grinning from ear to ear, not realizing the grip Monica had on her new man. Monica continued to wish Isaac and Jasmine the best, and thanked them for their anniversary wishes, all the while stroking Isaac's palm with her middle finger in a most subtle manner. Although her actions were extremely difficult to see with the naked eye, Isaac could feel every stroke from Monica. But Isaac had been drinking wine earlier and wasn't sure he was interpreting Monica's body language correctly. So, he smiled innocently to down play the situation and then looked Monica in the eye for further confirmation of her flirting with him in front of her best girlfriend on the down low. Isaac remembered the old saying his mother taught him as a young man: "Always look a person in the eye. The eyes never lie; they lead into a person's soul." As Isaac looked Monica in the eye, she didn't blink. She stared right back into his eyes as she continued to smile and stroke his palm with her finger that no one could see. Finally, Monica released Isaac's hand and said, "OK, let me make my rounds. You two look good together!"

Jasmine smiled once again and said, "All right then, we'll be here."

As Monica walked away, she began to greet the rest of her guests. Isaac couldn't believe what just happened. "My best friend's wife just made a pass at me!" he thought to himself in disbelief. Then he started thinking about all the times Darius got caught in a love affair. Isaac looked around the room to see where Darius was, and spied him over by the spiked punch bowl. "Be right back," he said to Jasmine as he walked over to say "hello" to Darius.

"OK, baby," acknowledged Jasmine. "Would you like me to make you something to eat?"

"Yes, thank you, that would be nice," Isaac replied.

Isaac began to work his way across the room toward Darius. He and Monica had a good-sized group now. R&B music was being played throughout the house. People were conversing and laughing with each other, but the music was loud enough to muffle out exactly what each conversation was about. Finally, Isaac made it to Darius. He was drinking from the punch bowl like it was water and he was on a desert. "What's up, man?" asked Isaac.

Darius looked up and saw it was Isaac, and he put down the glass of punch he was drinking. "You made it man," he said. "I'm so glad to see you, man." Isaac immediately smelled the familiar aroma of alcohol on Darius's breath. He knew Darius was already drunk or well on his way. "Whoa, take it easy on the liquor, buddy," warned Isaac. "You're going to be tore-up from the floor-up if you don't slow down on that alcohol, man."

Darius squinted his eyes and canted his upper lip as if to say, "Please, I'm a grown man. I can do what I want."

So, Isaac backed off a bit. "I'm just advising you to take it slow," he said. "No one is going to take your liquor, man. Save some for somebody else. This is your anniversary, and at the rate you are gulping down that booze, you're not going to make it to the end of the night."

Darius smiled and said, "Yeah, you're right, man. That's why I always loved you. You always kept it real and kept me focused."

Unfortunately, Darius had already consumed way more alcohol than he could handle. It was just a matter of time before he would be laid out on whatever was underneath him once his body collapsed. As time passed, Darius began slurring his words and his breath began to smell like "walking death."

"So what's been up, man?" asked Darius. "Did you come here with that woman who put it on you or what?" Darius started laughing, his body swaying from side to side as he fought to keep his balance. Isaac knew he was referring to Cynthia, so he immediately changed the tone of the conversation. "No man," answered Isaac. "I'm here with my new woman, Jasmine."

Darius opened his eyes wide in shock. "Jasmine locked you down that quick, man?" he asked, laughing at Isaac. "Man, you never cease to amaze me," said Darius, as he stopped laughing for a second. "First you get man-handled by Cynthia; now Jasmine put it on you and has you hen-pecked already."

Darius began laughing even louder. Isaac started to feel like a pushover because Darius threw in his face that Cynthia had her way with him and suddenly he was in a committed relationship with Jasmine. "I'm glad I can always amuse you, Darius," Isaac said sarcastically before walking away to go outside and get some fresh air. Even outside, he could hear Darius laughing deliriously. Isaac felt like Darius was mocking him.

Chapter 12

Double Dating

nce Isaac entered the garage back into the house, he could feel a slight breeze, for the doors were ajar. Isaac paced back and forth as he thought to himself, "I can't believe I told Darius about Cynthia and how that situation went down. From now on I'm going to keep my fat mouth shut. I'm too old now to be kissing and telling my most intimate episodes."

As Isaac contemplated with himself in the darkened garage, he heard a small noise in the corner. He strained his eyes to focus in on whom or what was there. The person lit a match to ignite a cigarette. The flame from the light illuminated Monica's face. The light went out after she puffed a few times to keep it lit. "Hey Monica," Isaac said. "How are you enjoying this wonderful party you and Darius put together? I think it's so wonderful you guys have been happily married for four years now."

Monica walked a little closer toward Isaac and began to talk softly as if she didn't want anyone else to hear her. The two were standing near a work bench underneath the garage's moon window. The moon was the only thing illuminating their position now. "It may be true about Darius and me being married for four years," Monica began, "but it's not completely true that I'm happy."

Isaac wanted to say something to change Monica's mind, but once again he was caught off guard. So, he just let Monica speak her mind. Isaac knew in the back of his mind that when a person is feeling indifferent sometimes all they need to do is vent to feel better. "The truth of the matter is, Isaac," continued Monica, "I know Darius cheats on me quite a bit, and the only reason I don't divorce him is because of our wonderful children. I grew up without my father and it sucked, so I promised myself when I was a teenager that I'd always allow my kids to grow up in the same house as the man I marry. It's a good philosophy, but things like happiness can be compromised if the person you marry isn't the one for you. So, I compromised my happiness for the sake of my kids. I haven't been happy with Darius since he gave me a sexually transmitted disease when we first got married. I saw the signs, but I just didn't want to believe it. Darius was walking around here with big blisters on his upper lip and bruises on his neck. He told me that sometimes when he gets a cold, he blisters up real bad and bruises appear on his body. I was stupid enough to believe him, but then I started burning and itching between my legs. At first I thought I just had a real bad yeast infection. But one day the symptoms were so bad I found myself dragging my back-side on the carpet to scratch the itching. And when I ran to the bathroom to relieve myself, I saw a dark green slimy substance on my underwear. The smell was absolutely unbearable. I don't eat seafood to this day because of that smell that permeated in between my legs."

Isaac smelled the alcohol on Monica's breath and took a step backward with his eyes frowned upward in disgust at what Monica was saying to him. "Monica, why are you telling me all this?" Isaac asked.

"I know Darius isn't perfect, but his positive attributes outweigh his negative ones. When you first got with Darius, you knew he was a player. So if he messed up at the beginning of your marriage, four years should be enough time for you to forgive him and move forward."

"Isaac, I know Darius is your best friend," Monica replied, "but, he's been having multiple affairs on me for years. He thinks I don't notice the signs, but I do. Most of the time, I turn the other cheek for our children's sake. Then sometimes when the kids are at the babysitter's, I argue with him about the infidelity. Darius has a serious problem keeping his mind and body out of the gutter. I don't think he has it in him to love me the way I need to be loved."

Isaac was stunned at what Monica was saying. He leaned on the workbench just behind him and placed both his hands on it. Isaac began to think deeply about what he could say to Monica to shed light on the situation. Monica could see from Isaac's expression that she was making him feel uncomfortable. So, she changed the subject. "Would you like a sip of my drink?" she asked. "It's really tasty. You can't even taste the liquor in it. I think it's vodka, fruit punch, and sherbet. Come on, try it," she urged.

Isaac thought perhaps taking a sip of Monica's drink would change the sour mood she was in. He wanted her to be happy on her anniversary. "Why not?" he said. "Give me that glass and let me see what is so great about this happy water." Isaac took the glass from her and took a sip. "Ummm, this is a tasty concoction you have here, Monica," he said. "Would you mind if I had just a little more?"

"Go ahead!" Monica replied. "Knock yourself out. There's plenty more where that came from in the punch bowl inside." Isaac took two more gulps from the glass. Monica watched him like a wolf ready to pounce on its prey. Isaac didn't catch the hard stare that Monica was giving him because he was more interested in the drink. As Monica watched Isaac drink from her glass, she thought, "That's it; drink it all up so you'll be all mine." Monica moved beside Isaac on the workbench as he continued to enjoy her drink, and bean talking about the latest in sports to occupy Isaac's mind. After about 10 minutes of drinking and conversing about the latest in professional football, Monica sensed Isaac loosening up a bit. His shoulders slumped downward and he began smiling more. He was no longer pausing between sentences or thinking about what he was going to say before he said it. He just said what was on his mind. Monica liked that. After Isaac emptied the glass, he said, "Hey, look, I am so sorry. I just dogged your drink. Let me go back inside the house and get you another drink, Monica."

Isaac attempted to get completely off the workbench he had been leaning on to go inside, but Monica placed her hand on his chest and slightly pushed him back. Isaac stopped smiling and looked deeply into Monica's eyes to try to figure out why she wasn't letting him get up. Monica then began to massage Isaac's shoulders. "Don't think about what's happening right now," she said. "Just relax and let go. Stop trying to do the right thing all the time and allow yourself to enjoy what feels good. Just allow your mind to rest, Isaac." She said in a calm, soothing tone, as she began rubbing the back of Isaac's neck. Isaac closed his eyes in the pleasurable moment. After Monica saw that Isaac was comfortable and relaxed, she moved in for the kill.

Monica had Isaac exactly where she wanted him. "Wow, I couldn't have planned this any better," she thought. The house is full of guests, and everyone's liquored up. The music is playing loud enough to muffle any noise indicating two people getting their groove on. My two-timing husband is inside, probably passed out drunk by now, and I have Isaac in the garage all to myself." Monica continued to rub Isaac in all the right spots. She slowly worked her experienced hands from Isaac's neck to his chest. Monica didn't realize this would drive him crazy; his pectoral muscles were very sensitive to the female touch. Once one of Monica's fingers brushed across Isaac's left nipple, he squirmed and let out a deep sigh in mere physical pleasure. Once she observed how good she made Isaac feel when she stroked his well – muscled chest, she rubbed it again to sexually arouse him and whispered very seductively in his ear, "That's it baby; just relax. Doesn't that feel good? It's just me and you in here and no one will ever know, OK, sweetheart?" Isaac was in pure ecstasy now and his blood began to flow to his groin. Monica had now seduced Isaac to the point of no return for the most intimate member of his body. Isaac didn't say a single word as Monica groped him. His silence was all Monica needed in order to know that she could become one with him. She pressed her body up against his and was very pleased to feel the rather large lump in his pants that she provoked to stiffen. Monica quickly reached over and grabbed a chair that had been folded on the side of the workbench they were on. She opened the chair and propped it against the garage door to prevent anyone from entering. Monica unbuckled her belt and kicked off her high-heeled shoes. Next, she took off her pants and placed them neatly on the spacious work bench in a most expeditious fashion. The moonlight illuminated Monica's nicely built legs and small waist line. As Isaac gazed upon Monica's wonderful physical assets he said under his breath, "Oh My God." Monica moved in seductively closer and the two began to kiss passionately. The more their lips massaged each other, the more their natural juices flowed. Before long, the two were at a sexual boiling point. Monica unbuckled Isaac's belt and aggressively pulled his pants to his ankles. Isaac was in full salute now. Monica placed her hands on his shoulders to brace herself. Then she hoisted herself upon Isaac perfectly, wrapping her legs around his waist, as he entered her. Isaac caught Monica's legs to keep them from slipping off his waist. He knew what he was doing was wrong. He wanted to stop in the back of his mind, but Monica's deliberate hip thrusts wouldn't allow him to drop her legs. Instead, he became determined not to let her go because the feeling was too splendid. He was strong and in good physical shape, but after about 15 minutes, Isaac's arm and back strength began to grow weary from supporting Monica's body weight. He began to breathe heavy from exhaustion, and attempted to ease Monica to the ground so she could stand on her own two feet. But Monica was in a zone. "Hold on for just a little bit longer, baby," she said, trying to reach her sexual peak. She knew if Isaac put her down, she might not get there. Isaac mustered all his body strength to hold Monica up. His legs and back began to tighten up, as he sweated profusely, straining with all his might to hold this woman up and steady. His body started shaking as his muscles began to fail, but Monica thought Isaac was shaking from ecstasy instead of exhaustion, and in turn became more excited. This was all Monica needed to finally reach her full potential, so she started trembling as she wrapped her arms around Isaac's neck. Isaac was through. He leaned back on the workbench and slowly released Monica's legs. As the two began to get their heavy breathing under control, Monica placed her feet back on the floor. They paused for a moment and looked at each other. "We need to get back to the party," Monica said.

Monica reached opened a cabinet above the workbench and pulled out a large box of baby wipes. "Here, take a few of these and clean yourself up," Monica said. "We don't want people to smell sex on us. Make sure you wipe off your face and chest."

Isaac began to stop thinking about the immoral act they'd just finished. "Monica's right," he thought. "I got to get myself together." Isaac began to move quickly. He took about six large baby wipes and started cleaning off the evidence of their forbidden, nasty act of fornication and adultery. About five minutes later, the two were significantly freshened considering what they'd just done. They quickly put their clothes back on. Monica fluffed her hair into a presentable style. They looked each other over, and nodded their heads signaling that they looked presentable enough to rejoin the party. "Isaac, you go out the garage from the front and come in the house through the front door like you just went to your car," said Monica. "I'll go back in from the interior door that we both left the house from." Isaac agreed. Monica removed the chair that she'd propped against the door and took a deep breath to try to relax. She didn't want to look like she'd done something that she wasn't expected to. Isaac pulled his car keys from his pocket and mashed the alarm button to activate and reactivate his car alarm to sell the idea that he was coming from his car. Isaac opened the front door to the house slowly as if nothing happened. The party was going strong. Everyone was talking and laughing. Guests were dancing in the living room, and the music was rocking the walls. Isaac started looking for his new girlfriend, Jasmine. As he walked through the crowd, some of the guests greeted him by saying, "hello" and shaking his hand as if he just arrived. Isaac cordially returned the greetings as he continued through the crowd. Finally, he spotted Jasmine and put on a smile as he headed toward her. Jasmine was laughing and talking with someone else, but as soon as she saw Isaac, her smile disappeared. "Where have you been for so long, baby?" she asked.

"I was having a man-to-man talk with Darius in the car."

Jasmine looked at Isaac in disbelief. Her eyes frowned inward and down toward her nose. "Darius has been over by the punch bowl all night, Isaac," said Jasmine. At that moment, Isaac knew that was caught in a lie, so he tried to make a strong comeback. "I – uh – went to my car and texted Darius to meet me outside so we could have our talk," he began. "I waited awhile because he told me he was on his way out. Like you said, baby, Darius has been at the punch bowl all night getting completely drunk and leaving me all alone in my car." Then Isaac thought to himself, "Way to think fast on your feet, Isaac," even though Jasmine still looked like she didn't believe him as she listened to Isaac's lame excuse.

"Yeah right! Whatever!" she said.

At that moment, Monica entered the living room and began conversing with various guests, smiling from ear to ear with a glass of the alcoholic punch in her hand. Jasmine looked at Monica and said, "That's funny; where have you been for so long? What a coincidence that as soon as Isaac returns to the party, you return as well."

Isaac began laughing nervously to make it look like Jasmine's implication of them being together was a joke. Monica became flustered and tried to create an alibi to throw Jasmine's suspicion off. "Girl, you are so crazy," she said. "I've been with Darius celebrating our anniversary."

Jasmine knew something wasn't right. She'd just caught Isaac and Monica in two off-the-wall lies. Jasmine's eyes began to tear. "I've been in the living room all night and Darius has been in the corner with his face in that funky punch bowl," she said, pointing at the corner of the punch bowl. Isaac and Monica simultaneously turned their heads in the direction of the punch bowl and observed Darius sitting next to it piss drunk. Darius was slumped backward in his chair with his head cocked back, his mouth wide open, and his eyes slightly shut. There was no doubt that Darius was completely wasted. Monica and Isaac looked at each other with guilty expressions on their faces as if they were caught red handed in the dirty deed they committed. Jasmine observed the two and asked Monica to see her hands. Monica looked confused as Jasmine slowly raised both of her hands to examine them. She noted Monica's fresh full set of nails. "Nice nails, Monica," said Jasmine. "Isaac would you come with me, please? There's something I have to know."

Monica was dumb-founded at Jasmine's actions. She had no idea what she was up to. Jasmine grabbed one of Isaac's hands, led him upstairs into the hall bath, and locked the door. "Why are you acting so strangely?" asked Isaac. "And what's with all the questions?" We're all supposed to be having a good time here. This is a party, after all."

Jasmine placed her index finger on her lips signaling for Isaac to shut up. Seeking the sincerity in her expression, Isaac stopped talking. "Take off your shirt!" Jasmine commanded.

"Take off my shirt!" he exclaimed. "What for, Jasmine?"

"So I can put my mind at ease," answered Jasmine, "because right now I could snatch you out of this house. Now take off your shirt,

Isaac!"

Everything was happening too fast for Isaac and he wasn't thinking sharply enough to put things together. "What harm can it do to take off my shirt in the bathroom with my girlfriend?" he thought.

Isaac unbuttoned his shirt and took it off. Jasmine placed her hands on his back and shoulders and began to examine him thoroughly. Isaac suddenly realized that Jasmine was looking for any signs of sex. Jasmine turned Isaac halfway around and saw the fresh fingernail scratches that Monica placed on his neck and shoulders while they were intimate. Jasmine let out a shriek of fury, like an injured canine, her eyes full of tears. "When you answered the door earlier today all you had on was some jeans and a t-shirt," she began. "You didn't have any scratches when you undressed to take a shower. Now, you have fresh wounds on your back! I am not retarded, Isaac! Monica put those marks on your body about 40 minutes ago, didn't she? That's why both of you were missing from the party!" Isaac knew he was caught red-handed. He had consumed too much alcohol and the night's events were far too dramatic for him to keep his composure and continuously falsely conjure excuses to bail himself out of trouble.

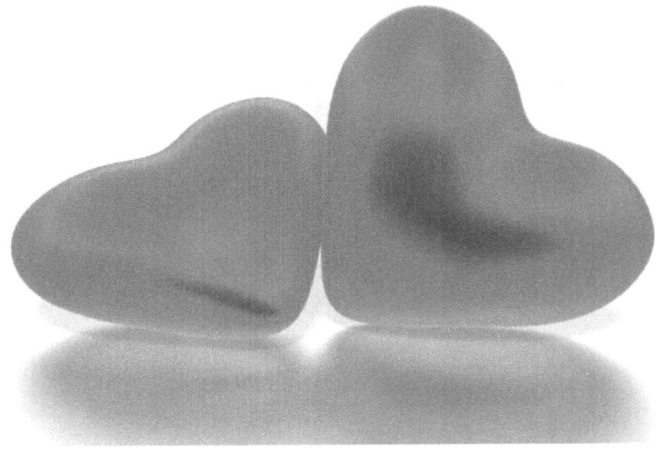

Chapter 13

The Pay Off

asmine and Isaac were still in the bathroom unraveling what happened that evening. Jasmine was slipping into sadness, and Isaac didn't know what to say to make her feel better. The sequence of events simply moved too quickly for him to react effectively. Jasmine was trying to remain level headed regardless of how disappointed she was. "How could you have sex with my best friend?" she said angrily. "We're only here together as a couple for a few hours and you can't even remain true to me that long. And then you have sex with my best friend at her house on her anniversary party!"

Isaac placed both his hands over his face and let out a deep sigh of dismay. Isaac was shocked that he would even be in a situation like this. He took his hands from his face and said, "Look, Jasmine, I didn't come here to disrespect you or sleep with anybody," Isaac began. "All I know is I had a few drinks, and then I went outside to get some fresh air. Before I could make it out of the garage, Monica was all over me like rice on meatloaf," he continued. "It was almost as if she had this all planned out, with the exception of getting caught. This has never happened to me before. Actually, there was only one other time I felt completely vulnerable, and that's the time I met up with that waitress who served us on our first date. She took advantage of me physically during a get-together we set up later. I mean she really humiliated me that night."

Jasmine frowned her face in disgust, her state of sadness transforming into rage. Her mouth and eyes scowled like a colonoscopy patient who hadn't received any sedatives. Jasmine began breathing more heavily as she realized Isaac was referring to the waitress she had classified as a low-down dirty tramp. Jasmine reflected on how cocky Cynthia was that evening and how she flirted with Isaac right in front of her. But what bothered her the most, she remembered, was how attractive Cynthia was. The volume in Jasmine's voice rose sharply as she said, "You had sex with that funky dog of a woman that waited on us on our first date? Boy, you move fast. It hasn't been that long since you and I went out on that date. I knew you were attracted to her. So, what do you mean she made you feel vulnerable?"

Isaac grew more and more embarrassed the more Jasmine yelled because he wasn't ready to tell her about what happened between Cynthia and him. He actually thought he may take that information to the grave, since Cynthia made him feel less than a man. But as he looked into Jasmine's eyes, he could tell that she genuinely didn't understand and needed to know the truth. So, he sighed deeply and placed his hands gently on Jasmine's. He guided her to sit on the toilet seat so he could give her all the miserable details. Jasmine aggressively pulled her hands away because she was thoroughly disgusted and didn't want him touching her. Isaac threw his hands in the air in a surrendering gesture to show that he was only touching her in peace. But Jasmine looked as if she'd just swallowed a dose of cod liver oil.

While Isaac knew he'd made a complete fool of himself, he also knew he needed to be man enough to be truthful with Jasmine, as she waited eagerly to hear what he had to say about what Cynthia did to make him feel so defenseless. "Cynthia and I met at a lounge after our first date," he began. "We had a few drinks. Then we danced to a few songs. Next we got some food to go. Afterward we went back to her place for a few more drinks. I was attracted to her, and she was apparently attracted to me. Before I knew what was happening, she was undressing me as if I were some kind of trick. I couldn't believe anyone could overpower me the way she did, and I'm so embarrassed by the entire incident." Isaac put his head down in shame as he recounted the story to Jasmine.

As Jasmine listened to Isaac speak, her anger lessened, although her emotions were mixed after she listened to Isaac's story. At first she was happy that a woman turned the tables and made the man a victim. But she also felt sorry for Isaac because the entire incident deeply disturbed him. Finally, she went back to being confused all over again. As Jasmine continued to mentally digest the story Isaac told her, after a minute or two of silence, she finally looked at Isaac in disgust and said, "Well, I am glad I found out early what kind of man you really are. The only reason I haven't ripped you apart is because I don't know you that well, and I haven't had the opportunity to fall in love with you. But I'm very disappointed in you, Isaac. I thought you and I had real potential. But, now that you slept with Monica, I don't think I could respect myself if I stayed with you. So I guess we'll never really know what was in store for us. Obviously, you're not strong enough to resist the temptations that come along with any beautiful woman you meet. I'm just lucky I found out so quickly. I hope you learned something from all this, Isaac. Now I need to go talk to Monica."

Jasmine exited the bathroom while Isaac stood there with his head held down like a toddler who'd just been caught with his hand in the forbidden cookie jar. He knew his inability to resist the temptations of a beautiful woman had gotten him into another bad situation. Although Isaac knew from past experiences that he would always encounter beautiful women, he felt in his soul that Jasmine was a good woman and that he'd ruined their chances of being together.

As Jasmine walked down the stairs to confront Monica about the findings of her brief, yet effective, investigation, the party was coming to an end. Guests were preparing plates for the next day, as the sound of foil being ripped in the kitchen echoed through the hallway. Guests were getting their jackets and saying their goodbyes. As Jasmine entered the living room, she saw Darius completely passed out on one of the sofas, turned on his belly, with his face over the edge. Jasmine noticed the plastic bucket beside the sofa under Darius's face to catch any vomit that would undoubtedly be coming from Darius very soon. At the moment, however, Darius was snoring heavily. Jasmine worked her way into the kitchen where Monica went. As she entered, the house was nearly depleted of guests. Jasmine looked Monica in the eye, deeply and sincerely. "Hey Monica, we need to talk," she declared.

The look on Jasmine's face told Monica that she was disgusted with her. Monica knew Isaac had let the cat out of the bag about what happened in the garage, but tried to play as if she didn't know what was on Jasmine's mind. "Sure girl," she said. "Did you enjoy yourself tonight? What's on your mind?" Monica tried diligently to smile at her best girlfriend, but her bottom lip was trembling nervously, anticipating Jasmine's reaction.

Monica quickly reflected on a time when she and Jasmine attended college together. Monica had opened her big mouth and got into an altercation with a cheerleader who was physically tougher than she was. When the cheerleader started dragging Monica across the gymnasium floor by her hair, Jasmine got the other girl in a headlock and punched her in the face four times, busting her lip and nose. Afterward Jasmine hip tossed the girl to the floor and began to stomp on her violently. So Monica knew that Jasmine knew how to fight, as she began to grill Monica. "I noticed you and Isaac disappeared this evening for about 40 minutes. Where did you guys go?" she asked.

Monica knew for certain that Isaac must have told Jasmine what happened because she could see the anger and concern in Jasmine's eyes. Monica made one last attempt to play the situation off by saying in a weak and nervous tone, "Girl, you are so crazy. Are you trying to imply that Isaac and I sneaked off together during my own anniversary party? Girl, you always had a vivid imagination. Come on and make you a plate to go, girl."

Jasmine raised her voice. "Do you think I'm stupid or something?" she said sternly. "I saw how you were looking at Isaac when you and Darius introduced him to me at your first cookout. I also sensed you were attracted to him during our conversations. Now at your own anniversary party, the two of you vanish for about 40 minutes after I tell you about our new relationship. I didn't want to jump to conclusions because you and I have been friends for years and I trusted you. So, I did a little investigation of my own just a few minutes ago. I examined you fingernails, which were freshly manicured. Then I took Isaac into the bathroom and looked him over. I found fresh scratches all over his back, shoulders, and neck that weren't there before we arrived. And finally, when I asked Isaac if you were the reason he was gone for so long, he couldn't even look me in the eye. That told me all I needed to know."

Monica stood with a deep daze upon her face in disbelief. She couldn't believe Isaac cracked under Jasmine's investigation. She also couldn't believe she got so caught up in the moment between her and Isaac that she left crucial evidence on his body. She didn't even remember scratching Isaac with such great force. Finally, she couldn't believe that Isaac wasn't savvy enough to invent an excuse or alibi about how he received the wounds, or even strong enough to look Jasmine in the eye and deny being with her. But at this point, Monica knew she was caught, and she wasn't going to make the situation worse by concocting a wild story to cover up the truth. "Look," began Monica, "Could you lower your voice? Darius might wake up."

"Oh, you don't want your husband to know he isn't the only player in your marriage, huh?" Jasmine responded sarcastically. Monica waved her arm signaling for the two of them to go outside on her closed-in patio for some privacy. Jasmine folded her arms in disapproval. Monica waved her hand more authoritatively to let Jasmine know she meant business. Jasmine reluctantly walked to the entrance of the patio, switching her hips from side to side slowly and making sure her high heels clicked as she walked, like a fatigued race horse walking across the pavement after a strenuous race.

As Monica entered the patio with Jasmine following behind her, she shut the door carefully so she wouldn't wake up Darius. Once the door was closed, Monica turned to face Jasmine. Jasmine's arms were still defensively folded as she waited for a response from Monica. Monica took a deep breath and exhaled slowly and began to speak in a sorrowful voice. "Please listen to me, Jasmine," she said. "I know I messed up big time, but I never meant to hurt or disrespect you. It's just that for years now, I've been very unhappy with Darius' affairs. Yes, he's a good provider for our family. He's even a decent father to our children, but at the end of the day, I'm the one who feels hurt, neglected, and unattractive. Over time, Darius continually made me feel like I wasn't enough woman for him. Do you know how embarrassing that is? When I go to work or run into family members and friends who know about the affairs, it hurts deep in my soul. It takes a lot of energy and effort to pretend I'm happy in my marriage. The truth of the matter is that I'm merely settling for Darius. He's a safe pick. When I got pregnant with our first child, I made the situation work for the best. I knew back then that Darius was a player. But I also thought as time passed that his responsibilities of husband and father would change him. I thought I was being smart by encouraging him to marry me because I thought he would mature and respect me more as his wife, rather than just his girlfriend or baby's mother. Boy was I wrong. I thought the added responsibilities would allow Darius to see what was really important in life. But even after four years of marriage and two beautiful children, my husband has probably had more sexual encounters with jump-off women than he's had with me."

Jasmine abruptly interrupted Monica. "What does Darius having affairs with other women have to do with you sleeping with your so-called best friend's man?" she asked forcefully. "You mean to tell me that because your husband is a cheating dog and has been for years, you decide to be with Isaac for a night? That makes absolutely no sense, Monica. You knew I'd been searching for a man with a stable background for a long time, a man who was educated, good looking, ambitious, responsible, and on the right side of the law. Isaac is all of those things. And until you put your envious paws in him, I thought he was an honest man that I could have something with. Now our relationship is over before it even had a chance to blossom because of the part you played in it. Was it worth our friendship, Monica? Sleeping with my boyfriend only tore us apart. You're no better than your cheating husband. What were you hoping to gain? Were you hoping to get rid of your complex that you're no longer beautiful because you have children and your husband can't keep his pants on? Or could you not stand to see me with a man you thought was a great catch? You were supposed to be my friend. You were supposed to be happy for me when I found a good and responsible man. Now I find myself watching out for tramps that I don't even know who flirted with Isaac, and it turns out to be you who stabbed me in the back. It's taking everything I have to keep from stomping you into the ground. So stay out of my life and don't talk to me again!"

Jasmine turned to walk off the patio, but as she exited the patio and reentered the kitchen, she found Darius standing next to the countertop. His presence startled Jasmine for a moment because she thought he was still asleep on the living room couch. But Monica and Jasmine were unaware that their voices were picked up over the house intercom and broadcast throughout the house. Jasmine knew from the expression on Darius's face that he heard most, if not all, the conversation she and Monica just had. Darius was leaning heavily on the countertop because his legs were still weary and his eyes were still bloodshot from the liquor. He held one hand over his mouth and his free arm wrapped around his waist. The deeply concerned expression on his face looked like he was attempting to solve an extremely difficult Chemistry myth. Seeing that Darius was about to go into shock, Jasmine called Monica's name gently so that she could come see the look on her husband's face. Monica approached the entry way to the kitchen where Jasmine was standing, cautiously, because she still wasn't sure whether Jasmine was going to beat her down for double crossing her. As Monica reached Jasmine, she was still focused on her with her mouth slightly opened. Jasmine, on the other hand, was intently focused on Darius and raised her hand and pointed at him. Monica turned her head slowly to see what had Jasmine in such a trance. When Monica saw the confused look on Darius's face, she almost lost control of her bowels. She knew immediately that he heard the entire conversation. Monica's heart began to beat harder and faster. Her hands started to tremble. Her stomach felt as if it were churning to make butter. Monica spoke nervously as an ex-con would after being found guilty of her third violent crime, punishable by death. "Are you OK, sweetie pie?" she asked to confirm her suspicions that she had been caught once again.

Darius looked up at the ceiling with rage permeating from his soul and let out a wild scream. "I can't believe this is happening!" he yelled loud enough to bring Isaac downstairs and into the kitchen. Isaac looked at Jasmine who had a look of defeat upon her face. Monica's eyes and mouth were wide open, as if she had just seen a ghost, and Darius looked like a pissed-off drunk who had just been robbed. Darius looked at Isaac and said in a slurred tone, "So I hear you had sex with my wife tonight. This was supposed to be our anniversary party, man. Well thanks a bunch; you're such a swell fella. You're such a pal."

Isaac shook his head from side to side and tilted his head slightly downward. Isaac knew that all four people standing in the kitchen knew he and Monica had been involved that night. Isaac tried to subdue the situation. "Look, Darius," he began in a sincere tone. "I didn't mean for any of this to happen. All I remember is having too much to drink tonight, and I went outside to get some fresh air. The next thing I knew, Monica came in. We had a few words ----."

Darius rudely cut Isaac short and finished his sentence. "And then you gave my wife a swell anniversary present," he interrupted.

Monica stepped in the middle of the room with both her hands raised to her shoulders in a gesture for everyone to calm down. "Look, honey, you had a lot to drink tonight," she said to Darius, "and I think it would be best if Isaac and Jasmine went home. You need some rest and we can discuss this in the morning."

Darius looked at Monica like she was the stupidest person he'd ever met, and responded in an agitated voice, "Woman, have you bumped your head or something? That was the dumbest thing I've heard all night and I'm drunk. No one is going anywhere until I say so."

Monica put her hands back to her sides and moved to her previous spot, with the look of "OK!" upon her face. Darius was still highly intoxicated and his coordination was terrible. His knees began to tremble and his face fringed up as is he sucked on a sour lemon. Isaac picked up on all the signs that Darius was about to attack him. Darius let out a drunken roar and charged Isaac to try to tackle him to the ground, but Isaac quickly side stepped him, and Darius' momentum carried him head first into the 52" flat screen Sony television set in the living room.

Monica let out a chilling scream, rushed into the living room, and laid eyes on her husband awkwardly sitting on one side of his body. The TV was completely smashed. Even though Darius had a slight cut on his forehead, he didn't feel any pain, or anything else for that matter, because of the alcohol. Isaac and Jasmine rushed into the living room to see if Darius was OK. When Isaac placed his hand on Darius's shoulder to try to help him to his feet, Darius let out a violent yell. "Get your hands off me! I can't believe this is happening! This was supposed to be a happy evening!"

Isaac backed away from Darius with his hands raised to gesture that he was only trying to help him up. Monica started crying, and said to both Isaac and Jasmine, "I think it would be best if the two of you left. Darius isn't ready to talk about anything right now because he's too drunk."

Chapter 14

Chain

Reaction

As Isaac and Jasmine turned slowly to leave the house, Darius was playing possum, still lying in that same awkward position he was in after his head bounced off and ruined the living room television. Considering how intoxicated he was, he still mustered up enough smarts to get Isaac to relax enough to turn his back on him. So while Monica was massaging Darius's head in an attempt to soothe him, Darius leaped to his feet and bum rushed Isaac once again. The problem was, he forgot to keep his mouth shut, and as he was charging Isaac, he screamed at the top of his lungs like a soldier charging his enemy on the battlefield. Isaac reacted quickly once again by stopping in his tracks and squatting to the floor. Not expecting Isaac to lower his level in such an instant, Darius practically jumped over Isaac, and slammed violently into the entertainment center. A piece of glass broke off deep into Darius's shoulder, and blood oozed down Darius's arm and spread over his shirt and pants. "Oh my goodness, we have to get him to a hospital," said a concerned Jasmine. "That cut looks bad."

"Man, will you just stop for a minute," said Isaac to Darius. "You're not doing anything except killing yourself. I don't want to fight you. On the contrary, I'm trying to put an end to a horrible night. I'll call the ambulance." Isaac walked briskly into the kitchen and dialed 911. Monica was crying so hard she began to dry-heave. She tried to slow her breathing down but almost swallowed her tongue in the attempt. Monica started making asphyxiating sounds as if she were going to cough up a lung. Jasmine ran to her assistance, placed her hands around Monica's shoulders, and guided her to a sitting position on the living-room sofa. "Just calm down, Monica," said Jasmine. "Everything is going to be OK. Just relax. An ambulance is on the way." Monica's choking slowly decreased, as did her rapid breathing. Jasmine continued to soothe her with words of encouragement and light rubbing on her upper back.

After about seven minutes, the sounds of emergency sirens were headed toward the home. "I'll direct them inside," Isaac said. He walked outside to meet with the ambulance crew.

Monica's breathing, as well as all her faculties appeared to be back to normal. Darius was still lying on the floor with the broken entertainment center on top of him, moaning in obvious agony as he pressed his hand firmly against his shoulder wound in a poor attempt to slow the heavy bleeding. Jasmine looked at Monica. "Are you OK, now?" Jasmine asked. "The ambulance is here and Darius will receive the medical attention he needs. I'm going to leave now and I hope everything works out for you guys."

Monica looked sorrowfully at Jasmine. "Thank you for all your support tonight and throughout my life," Monica replied. "You truly are a good person and a wonderful friend. I'm sorry for what happened tonight. You didn't deserve to be betrayed by me or anyone else. I hope that in the not-so-distant future, you can find it in your heart to forgive me. If not, I completely understand."

Jasmine walked out of the house and suddenly realized she had to wait for Isaac because he was the one who escorted her to the party, and her car was still parked at Isaac's. She immediately began thinking of how she could get a ride to Isaac's to retrieve her car without having to rely on Isaac for a ride. Meanwhile, Isaac was on the front lawn guiding the medical staff to Darius. "There was a party here this evening," he began explaining to the EMTs, and some guests had a little too much to drink. As a result, their handicapped coordination caused them to miscalculate the steps on the stairway and fall into the living room, damaging some furniture and sustaining injuries to themselves."

"You always know what to say, Isaac," replied Darius in a sarcastic drunken tone. "Did you think of that sorry excuse while you were outside? This isn't over between you and me. You have the audacity to come into my home, have sex with my wife, allow me to bust my house up because you are too punkish to fight me like a real man, and then go home as if nothing happened. Boy you must think I'm a sucka' if you think I'm going to let this slide."

The medical staff looked at Isaac with confused expressions on their faces. "Do you see what I'm talking about, guys?" he said to the crew members. "Some of us have had far too many drinks tonight, and this gentleman you have before you with the deep cut on his arm is one of them. I strongly suggest that you guys don't get too close to his breath because you, too, may need medical attention as a result of pollution damage. This same gentleman also fell through the TV over in the corner. That's why he has that gash on his forehead and may be delusional at this point." Isaac sounded reasonable to the medical staff while Darius continued to slur his speech and looked like an intoxicated clown. Needless to say, the crew took Isaac's word over Darius' and decided not to contact the police.

Monica remained quiet as Isaac won the medical crew over by remaining calm, while Darius began vomiting right before their eyes.

The crew began assisting Darius and asked Monica which hospital she wanted them to take him to for treatment and evaluation. As Monica gave the crew a detailed medical history, Isaac walked quietly out of the house like a smooth criminal escaping from jail. Once he was outside on the front lawn, he met Jasmine and now had to deal with the fact that their relationship was over before it even began. Isaac could see the disappointment on Jasmine's face, but he knew he had to take her back to his place so she could retrieve her vehicle. "We'll, that takes care of that," he said innocently. "I think Darius will be fine. He's going to have one heck of a hangover in the morning, though," continuing the small talk to feel Jasmine out.

"Yeah that glass went pretty deep into his shoulder and he'll probably have a nasty scar," Jasmine replied calmly. Isaac nodded his head in agreement as he walked to his vehicle and opened the passenger door for her. Jasmine stood where she was and put one hand slightly up and waved it from left to right gesturing that his chivalry will not be necessary. "No thank you, Isaac," she said calmly. "While you were inside sorting things out, I called a cab. It should be here any moment."

Isaac was surprised that Jasmine got another escort so quickly. Nonetheless, he tried to remain a gentleman. "OK, I'll wait here with you until the cab arrives," he said.

"No, you don't have to wait," she responded briskly. "I think I see the cab approaching now," she said as she pointed down the street. Isaac turned his head in the direction she was pointing, and they both saw headlights closing in. Ten seconds later, the taxi pulled in front of the house. Jasmine walked over to the cab and entered the back seat. Isaac watched her give the driver the address to where her car was parked. The taxi pulled away as Isaac stood by his car dumbfounded.

By this time, the ambulance crew had placed Darius on a stretcher. One crew member held an IV in the air as the team walked to the ambulance with Darius in the center. Isaac felt very sad inside because he knew a great deal of what happened that night was his fault. Monica closed the front door of the house and walked to her vehicle to follow the ambulance to the emergency room. As she walked past Isaac, she looked at him and shook her head as if to say, "This has been one crazy night!"

Isaac watched the ambulance drive away with Monica following. Still feeling really low inside, he entered his vehicle and drove home slowly. Somehow the ride home seemed longer than usual. Isaac began reflecting on all the details and events that took place that evening. He continued to replay each act blow by blow and thought about how he should have responded differently. Unfortunately, he couldn't go back in time and change what already happened. Isaac had to live with the decisions he made that night. As he pulled in front of his home, he noticed that Jasmine had already picked up her car.

Isaac pulled into his garage, exited the vehicle, and walked inside his house, which seemed particularly dark and gloomy that night. It was entirely too quiet inside, so he decided to turn on the radio. "If You Think You're Lonely Now," by Jodeci was playing. Isaac felt bad enough without that song beating him upside the head. He knew Jasmine had the potential to be a good wife and that he'd ruined any chance of ever marrying her.

Isaac walked over to his sofa and sat down as he listened to the song. He knew in his heart that he was once again a victim of infatuation, immaturity, and alcohol. First, he got drunk enough for Cynthia to man-handle. Then he got drunk enough for Monica to manipulate him into sex, even though he knew there was always an attraction between them. He just didn't know how deep. But he could still smell the alcohol on Monica's breath as she invaded his space in the garage, all the while Darius was gulping down the contents of the punch bowl in the living room. And if all that wasn't bad enough, his best friend, Darius, had to be taken to the hospital because of his actions. Isaac continued to listen to the radio as he fell asleep.

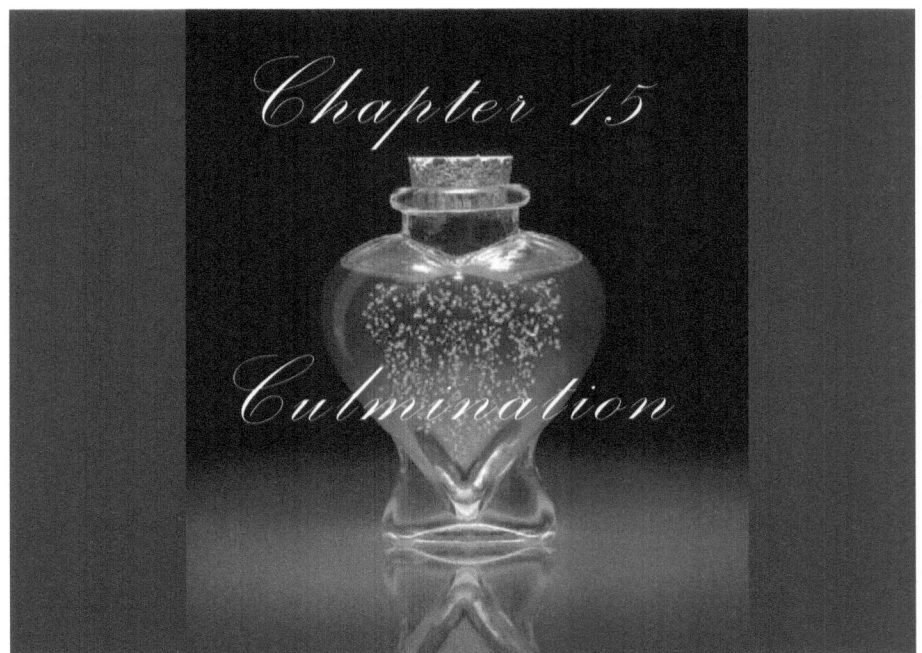

Chapter 15

Culmination

everal months passed. Isaac and Jasmine had not spoken to each other since Monica and Darius's anniversary party. Isaac managed to keep his head above water by not allowing himself to slip into a deep depression. He went to his job every day as expected and performed well. He managed to pay all his bills on time with no problem. He kept himself in good physical condition by exercising on a regular basis and maintaining a properly balanced diet. Nonetheless, Isaac continued to struggle with the psychological battles that followed him.

Isaac knew he needed some spiritual healing. He continued to attend church off and on, but even when he was there, he never really listened to the messages his minister was teaching. His mind always reflected on how Cynthia and Monica treated him like a piece of meat, and he had a difficult time coping with being used. Isaac promised himself that day that he would stop the nonsense in his life, and develop a stronger personal relationship with God. He was trying to be as realistic as possible. Isaac knew that with his hectic schedule that he wouldn't be able to attend church every Sunday. So he made the most important decision he could have, and that was to develop a strong personal relationship with God. To him this meant paying close attention to the lessons his minister was teaching, diligently seeking knowledge from the Bible, praying first thing in the morning for God's blessing on each new day, and praying at least once more in the evening prior to bedding down.

Up to this point, Isaac had taken his life for granted. He'd failed to acknowledge that everything he possessed was due to God's grace and blessings. Isaac had been living as he had pleased, disregarding others' feelings about his ultimate decisions. He reflected on how selfish he had been over his many years as a lover boy, taking advantage of any woman who came along who wanted more than just intimacy with him. He remembered how he played on their desire to have a meaningful relationship in order to get them into bed. He sold them false promises by giving the impression that he was interested in something more meaningful in order to break their guard down. In the end, all the women gave their bodies to Isaac without ever being married to him. One of the saddest parts was that Isaac never saw any of their positive qualities because he was too busy trying to sleep with them. In fact, he couldn't respect a woman enough to remain interested in her to discover her fine attributes as a person. This is why every relationship he'd ever had ended abruptly with each woman sitting at his front door wondering why he wouldn't let them inside. Yes, they were played.

Then Isaac thought about how the tables had unexpectedly turned on him. He thought about how he felt when he lost control of the night with Cynthia. Isaac knew he could have thrown Cynthia off of him, but he also knew if he physically resisted her, the two of them would have been brawling in that condominium of hers, the police would have been called, and he would have been arrested. And a domestic violence charge on his record would ruin the name and reputation that took many years to build. Isaac felt deep in his heart that he made the correct decision to reluctantly submit to Cynthia that evening. The only thing he regretted was not letting Cynthia know how he felt. He didn't know how to explain to her that what she did was wrong and why. Isaac assumed that Cynthia and others as well would view him as a softy for being too sensitive about it. He was already embarrassed when his friends laughed at him. Cynthia contacted Isaac several times but he ignored each call because he didn't know what to say. Cynthia was obviously interested, but he wanted nothing more than to forget she ever existed. He wished the incident hadn't happened. Isaac knew the only way that he would ever bring the situation to a close was to talk with Cynthia. Isaac prayed about the situation at church that Sunday. He asked the Lord to grant him the composure and choice of words that he needed to communicate effectively. When the minister finished his sermon, Isaac felt spiritually rejuvenated because he knew the power of prayer even worked for backsliders such as himself.

Isaac called Cynthia on the phone. Cynthia answered on the second ring. "Hey, Boo, where have you been?" she said.

"Hello Cynthia," Isaac said. "I know I haven't returned your calls and I apologize. I would like to meet with you on neutral ground to discuss why I've been avoiding you."

"Sure, no problem," she replied in a concerned tone. "Did you have a place in mind where you wanted us to meet?"

Isaac paused for a few seconds as he thought of a location with minimal distractions where they could listen clearly to one another. "Yeah, meet me at the coffee shop on New York Avenue and Fifth Street in about 40 minutes, OK?" he asked.

"Yes, that's fine with me," replied Cynthia. "I'll see you then." The two ended the call and hung up. Cynthia was excited that Isaac finally returned her phone calls, but she sensed that something was on Isaac's mind. Cynthia was completely unaware that her actions on their first date affected Isaac in a negative manner.

About 35 minutes later, Isaac pulled in front of the coffee shop and saw that Cynthia had already arrived. Her car was already parked in the rear parking lot, and she'd chosen a secluded table toward the back of the restaurant so they could have some private time. As Isaac entered, Cynthia waved her hand in the air. "Hey, Isaac, here I am," she said, smiling from ear to ear, delighted to see Isaac. Isaac returned a slight smile to merely acknowledge her presence. He walked over to her, and she grabbed his hand and led him to their table. Isaac didn't care for Cynthia grabbing his hand because she'd already taken advantage of him once. And since then, he'd developed a complex regarding women taking control of any situation he was involved in. The two sat down in their seats. "So, how have you been these days, Isaac?" Cynthia asked. "I have seen better days, but nonetheless I'm blessed."

The two ordered Cappuccino with some freshly baked cheese bread. As they waited for their order, Isaac began to speak to Cynthia in a mellow tone that radiated with deep sincerity. "Look, Cynthia, I wanted to meet with you today to talk about why it has taken so long for me to return your calls. The truth of the matter is, if I treated you the way you treated me on our first date, I'd be locked up for aggravated sexual assault." Cynthia sat with an expressionless daze on her face. She couldn't believe the words that were coming out of Isaac's mouth.

Just as Cynthia was about to respond, their order arrived. Neither Isaac nor Cynthia said a word because they didn't want anyone else to hear their conversation. Once the waiter placed their order on the table, Isaac thanked him, and the waiter turned and walked away. "What do you mean by that?" Cynthia said in a concerned tone. "I thought you didn't mind an aggressive woman in your life. I know I was a little assertive but not to the point of violating you."

"Cynthia, you were so liquored up that you were out of control that night," Isaac responded. "I physically resisted you, but you just would not be denied that night. You practically turned into a She Hulk. If I had resisted you with all my might, we would have been fighting in your loft."

Cynthia knew Isaac was telling the truth as he saw it. She began to feel sorrowful inside. "I guess this is why every man I've ever have been attracted to fails to return my calls," she said. "I was told a long time ago that I can be too aggressive. As a little girl, I was always a tomboy. I honestly didn't see any harm in being assertive while making love."

"That's just it," Isaac interjected. "We didn't make love that night. We don't know each other well enough to make love. All we did was have sex without any meaning behind it. Sure, it felt good to you, but to me it was one of the worse experiences I can remember."

Cynthia tilted her head down slightly. It was clear to Isaac that she was feeling offended. "The next time you meet a man you are attracted to, get to know him first," suggested Isaac. "It's OK to be old fashioned and not sleep with him on the first date. If neither of you can resist the temptation to have each other, take things slowly at first. There is nothing more unattractive than a woman who appears desperate. And take it easy on the alcohol that night. Not everyone can handle liquor responsibly. I'm not trying to preach to you because no one is perfect and we all fall short of the glory of God. But hopefully, I've given you some advice that will help you with any man you find attractive."

Cynthia understood and respected what Isaac said. "Well, I'm sorry for being overly assertive with you that night," she said. "I honestly didn't know I made you uncomfortable. The liquor had me on a roll. I'm glad we had this conversation, Isaac. Can we at least be friends?"

Isaac nodded his head in approval. "Sure." He extended his hand in friendship to Cynthia and the two shook hands. Isaac felt much better afterward. A heavy weight had been lifted off his back now that he'd expressed himself to Cynthia. Now she understood how her actions affected him, and he felt she would be more aware of her actions in the future. Isaac knew he had accomplished his goal in making himself and Cynthia better people. The two finished their order and conversed about other things. After a couple of hours, the two gave each other a friendly hug and a kiss on the cheek. They said goodbye and exited the coffee shop. They drove away from the parking lot knowing they'd learned a valuable lesson: Get to know your dates first, and don't go to bed with them just because you find them attractive.

Although Isaac felt good once again, he knew he had to make amends with a few other people who really made a difference in his life, namely Darius and Monica. Only a few months had passed since that fateful anniversary party, and he knew he was taking a huge chance by confronting them. But he was going to be a man about it; hopefully neither of them would be drunk. He wasn't quite sure how to approach the situation; he only knew the only way to achieve any closure was to communicate while everyone was sober. Not wanting to alarm Darius or Monica of his presence, Isaac decided not to call prior to his arrival. He didn't want a fight to break out between Darius and him. Nonetheless, he was ready to face whatever came his way. He just wanted closure; he hadn't intended to sleep with Monica or fight with Darius, but he had. So, Isaac made up his mind to confront them. He took a deep breath and exhaled slowly, and made a u-turn in the middle of the street to head toward Darius and Monica's house.

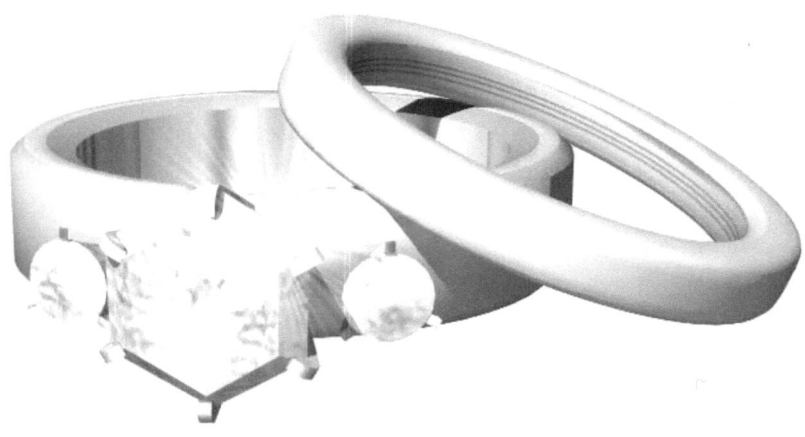

Chapter 16

The Power of Closure

saac pulled in front of Daris and Monica's about 25 minutes later, to talk about the horrible events that happened at their anniversary party. As Isaac exited his vehicle and secured it with the alarm system, he began having second thoughts about knocking on their door "Maybe it's too soon for me to come over here," he thought. As Isaac stood contemplating, Darius exited the house through the screen door. He looked at Isaac but didn't say anything for about 10 seconds. Isaac sensed from the blank expression on Darius' face that he was very surprised to see him, as if to say, "You've got some nerve coming to my house after you disgraced it."

Isaac broke the silence. "Hello Darius," he began nervously. "How have you been, man? I thought I'd stop by to check on your condition since all this nonsense took place."

"Oh, you want to stop by and check on my condition," he said sarcastically. "We'll aren't you just the perfect buddy." Darius turned his head slightly to the left and spoke loudly enough so that whoever was inside the house could hear. "Hey, Monica! Guess who stopped by to check on my condition?"

A few seconds later, Monica arrived at the front door to see who Darius was referring to. When she saw Isaac standing curb side by his car, her mouth opened wide in disbelief. It was obvious to Isaac that Monica was shocked and even embarrassed by his presence. She obviously didn't know what to say, so she didn't say anything at all. Isaac walked forward slowly. "I came by so we all could talk about this like responsible adults," Isaac said. "I mean we were all drunk that night and out of touch with reality. We all said some things we didn't truly mean and unfortunately we all did some things we all wish we could undo. But we can't change any of it. I know if I could go back in time, I'd change some of my actions that night. But we can only decide where we go from here and what we gained or lost from our poor decision making."

Darius looked at Isaac with a silly grin. "My man, Isaac, the philosopher," he said sarcastically. "You never cease to amaze me. So you want to talk about double crossing your best friend by having sex with his wife on the night they celebrated their anniversary. You want to go into specific detail about how you took advantage of the fact that I was drunk, by allowing me to swan dive into my TV and then allowing me to power drive my shoulder into a glass cabinet. OK, pal, let's go inside and have a glass of iced tea and discuss how all of this came about." Darius moved to one side on the front porch and opened the screen door for Isaac. Monica was watching Darius very cautiously because she wasn't sure whether Darius was seeking revenge against Isaac.

Isaac walked slowly toward the doorway to enter the house. As he proceeded forward, he could feel his heart pounding. As the anxiety was building in his system, Isaac began to meditate to calm his heart. As Isaac arrived at Darius's location, he could sense the tension, the anger, and the frustration vibrating from Darius' spirit and the anguish and shame that radiated from Monica. Isaac continued to walk fluidly into the house like a smooth cat in a night club. "Is it OK if we talk on your patio?" he asked. "I can hear your children playing upstairs and I don't want them to hear our conversation."

Darius looked at Isaac disgracefully and was about to say something but, Monica cut him off. "The patio would be a good place to have this discussion," she said.

As Isaac walked toward the patio, Monica placed her hand on Darius' arm in the event he should lunge at Isaac. She didn't want a fist fight to break out. The muffled sounds of two children running upstairs to the bedrooms as they played could be heard on the patio. When the three were finally inside the patio, Darius asked Isaac to have a seat and make himself comfortable, even though he was upset with Isaac, and the strained expression on his face told the tale. Monica guided Darius to sit on the sofa next to Isaac's chair. Darius spoke first. "So what exactly do you have to say about betraying me?" he asked angrily. "I would have never expected my ace of a friend to stab me in the back like that. After all the years and struggles you and I have been through, how could you allow this to happen? You crossed the line that should never be crossed between best friends, and I don't know if you can simply talk yourself out of this one."

"I'm not here to talk myself out of anything, Darius," Isaac responded. "I'm here to address a few issues that truly need to be brought to the forefront. First, I'm here to give you a formal apology for the entire incident. I am truly sorry for the part I played in the entire ordeal. Next, I would like to say that I was drunk and so was Monica. But we should have never had sex together. Now here's is the kicker; if you would have stopped having affairs throughout your marriage, Monica would have never pursued me or any other man in the first place."

Darius took great offense to Isaac's last statement. "Do not sit there and try to turn this into a blame-shifting session because we all know I did nothing wrong that night, except consume too much alcohol," Darius barked back.

"That's true," Isaac responded. "You didn't do anything particularly wrong that evening but the things you've been doing on many other nights are the root of the problems. Most people that know you and Monica are aware of your problem, Darius. People know you've been sleeping around for years. It's no big secret. Monica has caught you too many times with your pants down and your hand in the forbidden cookie jar."

Darius was becoming more irritated as he shifted his body on the sofa. But before Darius could respond, Monica said in a calm tone, "We'll, since we're telling the truth and doing some soul searching here, I think we should share some private information with you, Isaac. Darius and I have been addressing the root of our marital problems with our minister at church. Darius has come to fully understand that his cheating on me has caused a great deal of heartache and mental anguish. Even though the end result of me turning sexually to another man wasn't justified, I violated our sacred wedding vows just to get revenge. I wanted Darius to feel the hurt that comes along with a spouse who constantly has affairs. I also wanted to see for myself whether I could be intimate with the man of my choice, even if it only for one night. After giving birth to two beautiful children, I felt like Darius found me unattractive. And then there was the thrill of having an affair with another person. I've been intimate with Darius for six years, two years in dating and four in marriage. I saw other good looking men out there, but no matter how strong their charm was, I always remained true to Darius. I chose you, Isaac, to be the one I cheated with because I've known you almost as long as I've known him. You guys were always best friends. I felt so comfortable with you that it wasn't like I had been intimate with a complete stranger. I never intended to get caught, but I did and I'm no better than Darius for being untrue to me. I regret hurting my dear friend, Jasmine, because I know she really liked you, Isaac, and she saw real promise in being with you."

Darius had a disappointed expression on his face as he picked up where Monica left off. "Look, I know I haven't been the perfect husband," he began calmly. "My lack of will power has plagued me for years now. I know my cheating has taken a major toll on our marriage. Monica is a good wife and mother to our children, and she doesn't deserve my being untrue to her over and over again. Fortunately, Monica and I decided to start fresh after our anniversary party. I agreed to seek counseling for my addiction to sex, and Monica agreed to attend the sessions by my side. We both know it will be a struggle because I can't change overnight. But, I'm diligently working on my problem. They say God works in mysterious ways. But they also say 'what goes around comes around.' Years of infidelity led my wife to become intimate with you. I always knew in the back of my mind that my wife is attractive and could have just about any man she wanted if she put her mind to it. I just never imagined you'd be her choice, Isaac. I also never thought you'd sleep with Monica, no matter how alluring she was. All these years I've kept a watchful eye over the colleagues and certain friends and family members I felt would seize any opportunity to sleep with my wife, and it turned out to be the least-expected man in my circle to seal the dirty deal in having her for just one night."

Darius was really hurting now. The thought of another man being intimate with Monica was very stressful to him. Monica and Isaac could see the tears forming in Darius's eyelids. He fought diligently to keep them from falling. Isaac decided to say one last thing before he departed. "I'm glad this situation has made some positive changes in your marriage. I can't take back the deceitful part I played, but for what it's worth, I'm a better and more experienced person because of it. Darius, you and I have been friends for years. I don't know why all this had to happen, but as you said everything happens for a reason, and God works in mysterious ways. I am neither certain why this took place or whether God had anything to do with it. The only thing I'm sure of is that if it takes us to grow apart so you and Monica can be happy in your marriage, I'm all for it. It's also clear that both of you realize how much you truly love each other. I can see it in your eyes and expressions right now. I'm very happy that you guys didn't break up over all this nonsense. I wish you well and may God bless you and your family."

Isaac stood to his feet and extended his hand in friendship to Darius. Darius extended his as well, and they both shook hands. Darius gripped Isaac's hand very tightly in frustration and sorrow. Isaac knew that Darius was restraining himself from a physical altercation. As Darius released his death grip on Isaac and put his head down, a single tear drop flowed from one of his eyes. Isaac looked Monica in the eye and the two merely nodded their heads, letting one another know that closure was achieved. They both acknowledged their physical rendezvous was a costly mistake. Each knew there was a strong possibility that Isaac would never be part of that circle again.

Isaac exited the patio, walked smoothly out of the house, entered his vehicle, and drove away feeling completely vindicated. But as he continued to think about the conversation, he remembered the encounter he and Cynthia had at the coffee shop. He truly felt like he put a cap on each situation. Then, Isaac's stomach began to churn just like it did before he arrived. He realized there was still a missing piece to this puzzle---Jasmine. Isaac realized he hadn't spoken to the most innocent person involved in all this crazy drama, and that he needed to.

Isaac wasn't looking forward to meeting with Jasmine. He knew he'd truly hurt her feelings. He also knew if he didn't speak to her, he'd never have complete closure. As Isaac continued to drive, he began thinking of creative ways he could set up this meeting. So many questions entered his head: "Has enough time passed by for her to face me?" "Where should I meet her?" "Does she have a new man in her life?" and "Is she still in town?"

Isaac reached his house without having a clue how he would set this meeting up. As Isaac parked his vehicle and went inside, he sat down and poured himself a glass of red wine to unwind. He'd had a very stressful day, and he knew he had to be relaxed before he tried calling Jasmine. As Isaac stretched out across the living room floor, he began sipping his wine and turned on the TV because he thought it was too quiet and he got tired of listening to himself think. After a few minutes of watching TV and sipping wine, Isaac fell asleep where he lay.

Three hours later, Isaac woke up from his replenishing nap. Tired of trying to think of ways to arrange a meeting with Jasmine, he took the most direct approach he knew and simply called her. After three rings, he heard Jasmine's familiar voice. "Hello?"

"Hello, Jasmine," Isaac replied. "It's me, Isaac."

There was a brief moment of silence. Then Jasmine smiled and said, "Hello, Isaac, how have you been?"

"I'm doing OK these days, but I wanted to meet with you to discuss some matters that we didn't get a chance to resolve since Monica and Darius' party."

There was a moment of silence once again. Isaac sensed that Jasmine was thinking. Then she said, "I don't think that's such a good idea."

"Why not?" Isaac asked in surprise.

"I don't think my man would appreciate me meeting with my ex-boyfriend to discuss why we didn't stay together," replied Jasmine.

Isaac smiled to himself on the other end. He thought it was cute that she had moved on so quickly. At the same time, however, he knew he was the reason she had someone new. "Wow! You have a new man already?" Isaac said lightheartedly. "I guess it doesn't take you long at all to move on, huh?"

"No, not quite as fast as it does you to sleep with people's best friends," she fired back in utter cockiness.

"Look, Jasmine," Isaac said. "I didn't call to argue with you. I just wanted to discuss what really happened now that we're both sober."

"But that's not going to change the fact that you slept with my best friend while you were going out with me," Jasmine fired back. Clearly Jasmine was still bitter about the incident and his chances of meeting with her face to face were slim to none. Isaac knew if he were going to get any closure with Jasmine it would have to come over the phone.

"I know what I did was completely wrong," Isaac continued. "I didn't plan for any of that to take place. I have known Darius and Monica for years and never thought of having sex with Monica. Even that night, I didn't have any intentions of sleeping with her. I remember having a few drinks with you before we arrived at the party and then I had a few more with you in the living room. Then I went outside to get some fresh air, and Monica stopped me in the garage and talked about her relationship with Darius. She told me how unhappy she was that he had been cheating on her. Before I knew it, she was all over me. I resisted her, and she knew I was against her decision to carry out what she set out to do. I'm not making any excuses for my actions, but I was definitely provoked by Monica."

Jasmine laughed sarcastically and said, "Oh yeah, just like the incident between you and that funky waitress who served us on our first date? She seduced you, too, right?" Isaac knew Jasmine was mocking him. "Well it seems you're the innocent victim once again," she said.

"Isaac, assuming that what you're saying is true, you're not strong enough of a man to resist the temptation of any beautiful woman who throws herself at you," scolded Jasmine. "That is something you have to work on to become a complete man. You have to understand that just because you don't have any intentions of being with a woman, a woman may still try to force her will on you. If you are mentally weak, you will always get taken. It doesn't matter how physically strong you are; you have to develop a strong mind as well because the body will always follow the brain."

Isaac paused for a moment to digest what Jasmine just said. He knew her message made a lot of sense. "You know, Jasmine," Isaac began, "What you just said is absolutely correct. I really do need to strengthen my mind. I think that will come naturally over time as I mature. I think I can speed up the process by being mindful in any situation where I find myself alone with an attractive woman."

"That's just it, Isaac," Jasmine interjected. "Stop putting yourself in those types of situations. Walk away from the scene before things get too hot for both of you. I know I sound like a hypocrite because of what happened between us, but we shouldn't have ever been in that situation so soon in the relationship. All premature sex does is create confusion, false emotions, and a raunchy reputation, especially for women."

By this time, Isaac had a great understanding of what Jasmine was talking about. "I've learned a great deal from all of this and I apologize once again for the heartache I caused you," said Isaac. "I hope someday you and Monica can put this behind you and become friends again. You guys have known each other for a lifetime, and I hope one mistake will not keep you apart."

Jasmine laughed sarcastically once again. "Yeah, Monica and I have been friends for a long time, but people change," she said. "Monica is not the same person she was when she and I first became friends. She's in love with a husband who cannot love her the way she deserves, and until he can be true to her, she will never be the same. Her self-esteem is so out of whack because of Darius' infidelity that she threw herself on you to prove to herself that she is a beautiful woman. It's time for me to move out of her way and give her the time and opportunity to work out her marriage. Hopefully you will do the same with Darius and stay away so he can concentrate on Monica and what she deserves as his wife."

The two said their goodbyes and hung up. Isaac knew Jasmine moved on with her life and had no intentions of developing a relationship with him. He was fine with her decision because he had the greatest feeling of all---CLOSURE! Isaac had learned a great deal from his past experiences with women and whichever direction he chose to go, he was starting fresh, with more experience and a clear mind.

Chapter 17

The Moral of the Story

What's Really Good

he moral of the story is that no matter how many degrees and diplomas, or how much "street smarts" a person has, one must get involved in a Bible-based church and develop a strong personal relationship with God in order to become a complete person. Isaac was a very polished, educated, and successful individual, but alcohol consumption as well as the mixed emotions that go along with the territory of premarital sex and adultery got the best of him. As a result, he ended up creating tragic events in the lives of those he cared about.

While Isaac appeared to have a strong hold on life, he lacked the necessary maturity to make sound decisions when he found himself alone with a physically attractive woman. Even though he seemed to be a God-fearing man, he lacked the mental focus and strong belief system to keep his mind right in the world, and the only place we can find that focus is in the Bible (Basic Instructions Before Leaving Earth).

No matter how much worldly education Isaac had, he was no match for being seduced, enticed, and even abused. Only his belief in God allowed him to deal with the situation humbly by recalling the unfair ways he'd exploited women in the past. In the end, Isaac was only receiving a taste of his own medicine. If he had been a more complete person, he could have avoided the drama and the chaos he caused in his own life and in the lives of his friends.

The vast majority of young adults today regularly find themselves in situations where alcohol is all too easily at their disposal, even though the Bible warns against drunkenness. Unfortunately, many young people will and continue to drink alcohol irresponsibly, leading to the types of negative outcomes described in this novel. Throughout the book, overindulgence played a key role in costly decision making that benefitted no one.

Street smarts and common sense don't always go hand and hand. Isaac may have been charming and experienced in the dating game, but if he'd used more common sense while he was courting his prospective lovers, he would have realized that every action causes a reaction. But unfortunatley, he wasn't responsible enough to realize that once alcohol entered the picture, he could no longer control the mixed emtions and false beliefs that he helped create. So in essence, his street smarts backfired.

The Ultimate Alternative is to get right with God. If any relationship is going to work both men and women must have a personal relationship with the man upstairs. Even though no one's perfect, there's no reason we can't strive for perfection. Doing so means happier marriages and not sharing ourselves with multiple partners in meaningless relationships that cost us grief, heartache, and money. And when we have a strong personal relationship with God, we will have the desire and be able to seek the power necessary to break bad habits or addictions so that we can become productive spouses and respected leaders for our children.

www.ingramcontent.com/pod-product-compliance
Lightning Source LLC
Chambersburg PA
CBHW032151020726
47496CB00003B/818